5TO

HOLDING STEADY

Books by Stephen Schwandt

A Risky Game
The Last Goodie

STEPHEN SCHWANDT

HOLDING STEADY

Henry Holt and Company • New York

Published by Henry Holt and Company, Inc.,
115 West 18th Street, New York, New York 10011.
Published in Canada by Fitzhenry & Whiteside Limited,
195 Allstate Parkway, Markham, Ontario L3R 4T8.

Library of Congress Cataloging in Publication Data
Schwandt, Stephen.
Holding steady / Stephen Schwandt.—1st ed.
p. cm.
Summary: Seventeen-year-old Brendon tries to come to terms with
overwhelming grief, anger, and guilt during the first family
vacation after the accidental death of his father.
ISBN 0-8050-0575-7
[1. Death—Fiction. 2. Fathers and sons—Fiction. 3. Family
problems—Fiction.] I. Title.
PZ7.S39955Ho 1987   87-31687
[Fic]—dc19   CIP
                                               AC

First Edition

Designed by: Victoria Hartman
Map drawn from an original kindly provided
by the Washington Island Ferry Line.
Printed in the United States of America
10 9 8 7 6 5 4 3 2 1

ISBN 0-8050-0575-7

For family—Karen, Reed, Andrew
With special thanks to
Marilyn Marlow and Mary Cash

Come, my friends.
'Tis not too late to seek a newer world.
To strive, to seek, to find, and not to yield.

Tennyson, "Ulysses"

Washington Island – Door County

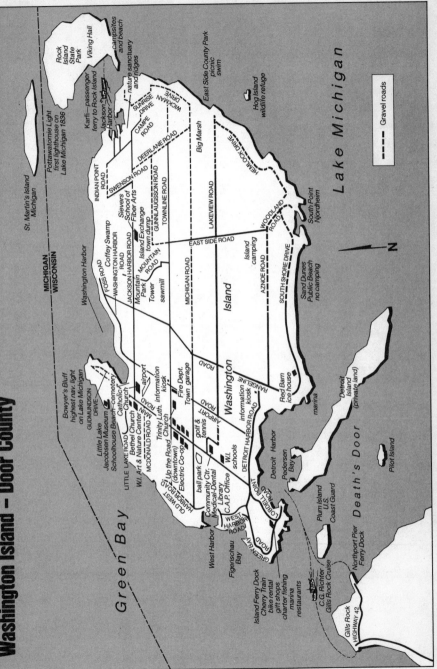

St. Martin's Island
Michigan

MICHIGAN
WISCONSIN

Green Bay

Rock Island State Park

Viking Hall

Pottawatomie Light
first lighthouse on
Lake Michigan 1836

Karfi– passenger
ferry to Rock Island

Jackson Harbor

campsites and beach

nature sanctuary and ridges

SUNRISE DRIVE

WICKMAN DRIVE

CAMPE ROAD

DEERLANE ROAD

Big Marsh

East Side County Park
picnic
swim

Hog Island
wildlife refuge

Lake Michigan

HEMLOCK DRIVE

Bowyer's Bluff
highest nav. light
on Lake Michigan

GUDMUNDSON DRIVE

Little Lake

Jacobsen Museum

Schoolhouse Beach–cemetery

Bethel Church

LITTLE LAKE ROAD

W.I. Art & Nature Center

MCDONALD ROAD

Up the Road (downtown)
Electric Co-op

ball park

Community Ctr.
Medical–Dental

Library

C.A.P. Office

West Harbor

Figenschau Bay

GREEN BAY ROAD

Island Ferry Dock
Cherry Train
bike rental
gift shops
charter fishing
marina
restaurants

C.G. Richter
Gills Rock Cruise

Gills Rock

HIGHWAY 42

Northport Pier
Ferry Dock

Plum Island
U.S.
Coast Guard

Pilot Island

Detroit Island
(private land)

Death's Door

Pedersen Bay

Detroit Harbor

DETROIT HARBOR ROAD

W.I. schools

golf & tennis

Trinity Luth. Church

Fire Dept.

Town garage

airport

information kiosk

Catholic Church

MAIN ROAD

AIRPORT ROAD

OLD WEST HARBOR ROAD

WEST HARBOR ROAD

LOBDELL POINT ROAD

RANGELINE ROAD

information kiosk

Red Barn
ice house

marina

Sand Dunes
Public Beach
no camping

SOUTH SHORE DRIVE

AZNOE ROAD

Island camping

MICHIGAN ROAD

Washington Island

EAST SIDE ROAD

LAKEVIEW ROAD

TOWNLINE ROAD

GUNNLAUGSSON ROAD

MOUNTAIN ROAD

town dump

sawmill

Mountain Park Tower Road

Island Exchange

JACKSON HARBOR ROAD

WASHINGTON HARBOR

FOSS ROAD

SWENSON ROAD

Sievers School of Fiber Arts

Coffey Swamp

INDIAN POINT ROAD

Washington Harbor

Washington Harbor

South Point
Njordheim

WOODLAND ROAD

N

---- Gravel roads

HOLDING STEADY

1

Seventeen-year-old Brendon Turner woke up to the sound of running water. He took a deep breath and stretched. Then he let himself relax and remember—this was the morning, finally. He rolled out from under the single sheet covering him and shuffled to the bathroom, where his little brother by nineteen months, one inch, and twelve pounds was shaving.

"W'cha doin'?" Brendon mumbled.

"Maturing," Ross answered, without breaking his concentration. His hand remained steady as he completed the first upward strokes.

"What?" Brendon said, combing back his thick, straight blond hair with his fingers.

"*Maturing.*" Then with his voice unnaturally deep, Ross explained, "You know, growing up."

"Aw, c'mon. There's more hair on the bathtub soap."

Ross laughed. "I'm further along than you think, pal. Besides, if Farber is doing it, there's no sense in me waiting."

"Farber shaves?" Brendon asked. "Every day?"

"Naw. Once, twice a week. Whenever he needs to relax . . . and think."

"Farber thinks?"

"He says it feels good."

"Thinking?"

"Naw. *Shaving.*"

"Oh."

"It does feel good."

Nearly awake now, Brendon had become fascinated by his brother's razor work.

"Where'd you get the stuff?"

"The *stuff*. You'll have to be more specific."

"The razor and cream, obviously," said Brendon, who shaved electric. "Is it Dad's?"

"Yeah . . . that okay?"

"Where'd you find it?"

"It's been here all along," said Ross, pointing to the cabinet under the sink.

Brendon hesitated, then said, "Maybe you should leave it alone, buy some for yourself."

"Why?"

"It's not yours."

"So?"

"So it's not yours." In the tense pause that followed, Brendon could see it coming, another *scene*. He'd just begun to realize how many of those he had caused this spring. He didn't want one today. It might ruin everything again.

By now Ross was putting the shaving equipment back where he'd found it. "Farber was right," Ross said brightly, stroking his chin. "It *feels* good . . . even without a blade."

"You didn't use a blade?"

"Naw. Not the first time. Never the first time. Farber says you've got to master your technique and style with a dull run before you take the Big Risk."

"Farber's been doing a lot of thinking. I hope it hasn't been a strain. By the way . . ."

2

"Yeah?"

"Since Farber's so grown-up now, you might ask him something."

"Yeah? What?"

"Ask him if he knows the difference between a fox and a pig."

"The difference between a fox and a pig," Ross repeated. "What if he doesn't know the difference?"

"The difference is fifteen beers."

Ross whooped so loudly Brendon winced.

"Control, *control*," Brendon said, smiling. "Mom's asleep."

Still, Brendon had done what he intended. He had gotten the day started on a good note. He'd been pulling the others down long enough.

All spring he'd provoked his mother and brother. But he had felt strangely driven to remember and to make them remember. Make them feel his anger and frustration. So whenever they seemed happy, acting like the worst was over, Brendon challenged them.

Easter break was a prime example. His Uncle David, his father's younger brother, asked them to join his family for a Florida vacation. "My treat," Dave had said. "It would do you good to get out of Minneapolis awhile."

When the others jumped at the chance, Brendon held firm. He announced to his mother he was staying put because going to Florida was a stupid, escapist thing to do. Of course, Anne wouldn't dare go without him. So she refused his uncle's offer. By the end of that gray, rainy Easter week, they all were depressed, but Brendon didn't care. In his mind, it was how things had to be.

Today, though, he'd promised himself to do whatever he could to make things work. The three of them were about to

take a summer trip to Washington Island. They were sched-
uled to stay at least a month on that relatively undeveloped
haven just six miles off Wisconsin's Door Peninsula, the
"thumb" of the state.

The last and only time they'd gone there as a family was
years ago. Brendon had been nine, but he still had vivid
memories of the long drive. His mother and father had
shared the driving then.

Now that option no longer existed.

2

While Ross got dressed, Brendon walked to his mother's room to wake her. Standing in the doorway, he watched her breathing evenly but very lightly. He was glad to find her asleep, and he didn't want to disturb her.

He glanced around the room. When he spotted the blowup of a picture taken while his dad emceed the faculty Christmas party, he went rigid, trying to repress the dark pain. But it shivered, swelled, then surfaced, and the sad truth declared itself once more—his father, Michael Thomas Turner, was *dead*.

Dammit, thought Brendon, *he* should be waking her up. In fact, he should be up already and waking *me* up.

It happened last February 7th, parent conference night for Michael Turner, a social studies teacher. Outside, a vicious wind, snow, and ice storm was attacking the highways.

Brendon had heard his dad phoning the district office, asking, "Could sanity please prevail and conferences be postponed?" Michael had listened a moment, said, "Yeah. Uh-huh. Look, I *know* it constitutes our primary public relations effort, but—" He listened some more. His last words were, "I'll try, that's all I can say."

Then he put on one of his best suits, his storm coat, scarf, and gloves, and marched out the door. Brendon wanted to call him back, but he hesitated and was too late. Michael had already run to his car, an old VW. Seeing that, Brendon panicked and finally raced to the door, pushed it open, and hollered, "Take Mom's car! Take the Pontiac!" But Michael waved off the suggestion and disappeared inside his precious once-golden, now rust-ravaged "limited edition" Sun Bug. Brendon's last words were, *"No. Don't."* For the vehicle was a school joke.

As long as Brendon could remember, none of his dad's colleagues would ride in it, not even to lunches, let alone workshops or athletic events. Michael's department members had dubbed his VW "the Death Car" because of the Beetle's perfect inability to sustain collisions of more than .03 miles per hour.

And though Michael kept insisting that the Bug was really "a high-performance testimony to German engineering," he went along with the kidding. He even had the initials "D.C." stenciled in black on the trunk, with a small skull and crossbones separating the letters.

But that snowy night the joke ended. That night the Bug spun out of control on a patch of freeway ice, then rolled, battered, and crushed itself.

Anne, Brendon, and Ross first became frightened when the school secretary called two hours after Michael had left home. She asked if he were really coming in. During the next hour they received another call, from the police.

Brendon had dozed off by then. The pacing, the anxiety, the wait had worn him down. But the ringing phone and his mother's scream made him sit bolt upright in bed. He shouldn't have fallen asleep. He should have been *out there*, doing something, something to stop it from happening. But instead, he had hidden under his covers like a scared little kid.

Soon the highway patrol arrived.

Then the neighbors.

Then a cousin of his mother's who lived close by.

Then the minister.

Then . . .

For the first weeks following Michael's death, friends and relatives tried to keep them active. Ross had behaved best. He gave the impression he was coping and ready to continue with his life. Maybe he was. And that too angered Brendon. Once, after hearing Ross laugh through a long phone conversation, Brendon had complained, "You don't care at all that he's dead. You just think of yourself."

"He is dead," Ross had replied, nodding. "And you know what? He's going to stay dead."

"So you just chuck it and move on."

"That's me, huh?"

"How you're acting."

"Brendon, I don't need you to bring me down. It's hard enough, okay? I miss him as much as you."

"Then act like it."

"You mean be like you? Go hide in my room? Quit everything? Forget my friends? You didn't even make the prom, stood up Lisa—"

"I didn't stand her up."

"Ditch her two weeks before, same thing," said Ross.

"Shut up!" Brendon had yelled, close to making it a fight. "Stop."

"You stop," Ross answered. "Stop playing games and get with it."

"What about *you*?" Brendon replied. "That's the point. What are you doing for him?"

"I'm doing exactly what he'd want me to do."

"Yeah? What's that?"

"I'm working hard in school. And I'm trying to be best at something we both cared about."

"Basketball."

"Why not?"

"Dedicate your career to old Dad."

Ross gave himself a few seconds before responding. Then he said, "You should quit this now, Bren. We're going nowhere."

"That's right," Brendon had said as he stalked out of Ross's room.

Alone, Brendon had done other things, strange things. Once, he had taken his mother's car and driven to the exact spot where his father had been killed. The place was at the bottom of a ravine where the freeway rose to cross the Mississippi River. Michael's car had stopped rolling at the river's edge. Brendon had parked illegally on the shoulder and slid down the snowy embankment on foot. He had stood at the spot until a highway patrolman called down to him, told him to climb back up, move his car, "get the hell going."

Later that same day, Brendon also located the junkyard where the Sun Bug had been taken. He found the car, and the sight of it made him sick. On the shards of windshield glass still in the frame, Brendon saw frozen drops and streaks of his father's blood.

• • •

As for Brendon's mother, a clinical nurse, she seemed numb most of the time. She would sit through meals, apparently listening to the conversation, but eat nothing and say as

8

little as possible. Then the tears would come. Once she said to Brendon, "I'm a *nurse*. I know about the grieving process, academically. But for myself, emotionally . . ." She trailed off and started weeping again.

It had been mid-May when Anne first mentioned a return trip to Washington Island. She'd already run the notion past her father, who'd promised to help with the planning. Brendon was alone with Anne after school one day when she told him about the idea. "It might be good for us. It was where we sort of started."

"You and Dad."

"All of us."

"So maybe," Brendon continued, guessing her thought, "it'll be a good place to start over." Brendon's indifferent tone let Anne know he didn't think the trip would solve anything.

"It could be the change you need."

"And I'm the one who needs changing."

"Brendon, I worry—"

"Don't," he had cut in. "You want to go, fine."

"Will you go with me?"

Brendon waited. Finally he said, "I don't know."

Anne stared at him, her mouth a little pinched. Brendon realized she was struggling not to tell him off. But maybe that's exactly what he needed. Maybe this trip would be the kick that got him going again.

Instead of nagging, Anne shared information with Brendon. She told him how his Grandpa Carl, a surgeon in Milwaukee still practicing at sixty-seven, was checking around for a good place to rent on the island. The very next week Brendon's Grampa phoned to say they were welcome to use the vacant cottage of a very busy cardiologist friend.

Then Anne made another positive move. She wrote to the

famous Sievers School of Fiber Arts and got herself enrolled in some intensive day-long weaving classes. When her acceptance notice from the island arrived, she showed it to Brendon and said, "I promised myself that someday I'd go back there and do this."

Brendon nodded. "Okay," he said. "Let's all escape."

So the trip was on.

• • •

His mother stirred.

Brendon caught his breath, pulled himself together, said, "Mom, gotta get up, okay? Time to go."

"Is it?" she asked dreamily, slowly opening her eyes. "Is Ross awake?"

"Uh-huh. So c'mon."

"Give me ten minutes. Have some juice. And if you really love your mom, please make a pot of coffee. All right?" With her eyes closed again, she smiled.

"I'll take care of it," said Brendon. "Ten minutes?"

"Promise."

Brendon walked back to his room. He was holding steady again.

3

They were on their way by half-past seven, with Brendon driving the first leg. The car sagged a little under the weight of a full load. The trunk and top carrier were jammed. On a rack bolted to the back bumper hung two ten-speed bikes.

There was little talk during the first four hours of driving. Both his mother and brother slept. This allowed Brendon to think about the past year. He tried to sort out what was important and what wasn't. He was surprised to discover how little some of his big concerns mattered to him now. Take football, he thought.

His father had always encouraged his sons to be interested in sports. With "hard practice, pure motives, and unfailing discipline," he had said, they might also experience "High Times—those intensely satisfying moments when you *become* what you're doing."

Brendon recalled how much his father had admired Ross's shooting form in basketball. Even before he left eighth grade, Ross had a flawless jump shot. Once, after watching Ross beat Brendon with a twenty-foot bomber, Michael had yelled, "It's perfect, kid! It's *pure*!! And you practice right every day, it'll never spoil."

Brendon wondered what he had that would never spoil.

What could he do perfectly? His father had never told him. And he hadn't figured it out on his own.

Brendon knew he didn't understand everything about Michael's ideas, but he was fairly sure he'd experienced at least one of those moments his dad valued so much. It happened this year in football. Michael had never actually said it was the real thing. In fact, Michael hadn't even attended the game; he'd been on "dance duty" at his school that Friday night.

As a junior wide receiver on Moorland's powerful team, Brendon wasn't the fastest member of the pass-catching corps, but he made up for his lack of foot speed by being clever, quick, and precise when running his patterns. He also had strong, sure hands. Brendon's moment came on the opening play of the first game of the season against Westpark, Moorland's chief rival for the conference championship.

In an attempt to surprise Westpark and get on the board early, Coach Grant sent Brendon on a slow-hook-and-go sprint down the left sideline. When Brendon cut from his route, slipped past his defender, and looked back over his right shoulder, the perfectly thrown ball spiraled into his hands and he raced the final twenty yards untouched into the end zone. There wasn't a Westpark player within ten yards of him.

That touchdown won the game for Moorland. But it was also a false indicator of Brendon's potential as a player. After the Westpark game, he caught only eight more passes in the next nine contests, none of them for touchdowns, none remotely as satisfying as the first.

Still, Michael suggested that maybe the punishing season was worthwhile, just for that one play—"Geez, I wish I'd seen it," he had said. Brendon wasn't so sure the gain was worth the pain.

12

After Michael's accident, Brendon could no longer enjoy any competitive team sport, especially football. But Brendon thought he could easily explain Ross's continuing dedication to basketball—it wasn't just something his brother did, it was something he had *shared* . . . with Michael.

Now even the laid-back life of a Moorland High track team member held no appeal for Brendon. Coach Foster's "come as you are and do your own thing" approach didn't interest him, either.

"You're not going out for *anything*?" asked Scott Ryan, a fellow flanker and a sprinter on the track team.

Brendon shook his head.

Later, nobody said a word when Brendon resigned from the lettermen's club and the National Honor Society. But when he went to the guidance office to drop Psychology I-A, a pre-college research and discussion class, his counselor, Mr. Cavanaugh, said, "You're withdrawing too much, Brendon. Is there some way I can help? Have you considered sharing your feelings with one of our therapy groups?"

"Losers!" Brendon had snapped, surprising himself with his reaction. He stood up then, mumbled a quick "Sorry," and hurried out of the office. The guy couldn't possibly understand, thought Brendon. Not in a million years.

• • •

Brendon had been thinking so deeply that he was in Wausau, Wisconsin, before he knew it, eating his late-morning hungry-man breakfast in a daze. Afterwards, Brendon's mother took the wheel. She seemed to become more and more animated the closer they got to Door County. All of them did, even Brendon.

While they were slowed by stoplights in some of the small towns along Highway 29, they made up for lost time by taking the freeway bypass that skirted Green Bay.

"When I was a girl," Anne said, "and we came up here from Milwaukee, we had to follow the highway right through the city. It twisted and turned and always seemed to be under construction. One of the highlights was passing by the Charmin Paper Company. The last time, though, somebody had spray-painted something across the side of the building. It was a rather nasty rumor about Mr. Whipple."

Ross laughed. Brendon smiled.

• • •

Within an hour they had also bypassed Sturgeon Bay and were easing through the resort towns most tourists think of as being Door County. Starting in Egg Harbor and then Fish Creek, Ephraim, Sister Bay, and Ellison Bay, Brendon was fascinated by the cluttered but carefree resort atmosphere of the bayside villages along Highway 42. Ephraim reminded him of the New England coastal towns he'd always admired in travel magazines.

As they followed the highway up the shore and through Ephraim, Brendon watched some hardy windsurfers and Sunfish sailors braving the elements. He envied them.

"We're almost there," Anne said. Looking at the whitecaps on Green Bay, she added, "I hope it's not too rough to cross."

"What if it is?" asked Brendon.

"When it's rough, but not too rough, the ferry leaves from Northport, on the other side of the peninsula. Otherwise they may still be using the Gills Rock pier. Grampa said the whole operation was moving to Northport permanently. We'll have to see when we get there.

Ross asked, "What happens when it's way too rough?"

"I don't know. I've never seen it that rough."

4

It was rough enough for a Northport departure. While waiting in line to board the ninety-foot flat-bottomed ferry, *Robert Noble*, Brendon sat quietly. Slow drumroll breakers crashed against the massive concrete pier.

"That boat looks big enough," said Ross, "but I think this is still gonna be bad."

"Maybe," Brendon said.

"No maybe. Look at 'er rock now . . . and it's tied up!"

Brendon looked beyond the ferry to the stretch of water separating them from Washington Island, the Porte des Morts Strait. He said to himself, Well, there it is, the passage Michael had spoken about. He began to remember the first time he crossed it with his father.

It was rough that day, too. The huge waves had fascinated Brendon, scared him. But Michael took advantage of Brendon's anxious interest. He impressed him with a story about the naming of Porte des Morts, Death's Door. Michael began it all with, "At least we're not going by canoe, boys."

"What d'you mean?" Brendon had asked.

So Michael told him.

Porte des Morts, Michael had said (ever the history teacher), came from an old Indian legend. One version

15

claimed that very early in the seventeenth century, war-loving Winnebagos came to Door County but found that the peninsula was occupied by peace-loving Potawatomis. Though the Potawatomis offered to share the land with the intruders, the Winnebagos wanted it all to themselves. So they began destroying Potawatomi villages, chasing the Potawatomis straight up and off the peninsula. The Potawatomis found refuge on Washington Island, which was then inhabited by the Menominees. But the Winnebagos weren't satisfied. They made plans to attack the island too.

The Potawatomis learned of the Winnebagos' plan and decided to run no farther. Instead, they plotted a counter-offensive. Their best warriors were to leave the island, cross the strait at night, and catch the Winnebagos unprepared. First, they sent three scouts to find a safe landing place. Once they chose a location, the three were to build a signal fire on the bluff above the site. Then the invasion would begin.

But the scouts were caught and tortured by the Winnebagos. Two of them were burned to death in front of the third. This last scout had already endured several savage beatings. He finally broke down and revealed the Potawatomis' plan.

The next night the strait was filled with huge swells. The Winnebagos found a treacherous run of rocky shoreline and built the signal fire above it. Nearly three hundred Potawatomis in eighty canoes began to cross the lake.

During the crossing, a sudden squall trapped the Potawatomis. They couldn't turn back. Against all odds, many of the invaders survived the trip, only to be thrown onto the sharp limestone rocks and sheer cliffs guarding the peninsula. Most died there. The few who landed were soon tomahawked or stoned to death by the Winnebagos.

To make sure that no Potawatomis survived anywhere, the Winnebagos had sent an invasion force to attack the island. But they too were caught in the storm. Canoe after canoe capsized until all the Winnebagos had drowned.

Early the next morning, the Winnebagos on the peninsula saw the corpses of their own warriors and their canoes. Soon Winnebago bodies were washing ashore along with the Potawatomi dead. The Winnebagos then named the strait "Door of Death." Later, French missionaries translated it as Porte des Morts.

Then Michael had told another Death's Door anecdote.

"Once," he began, "some high school buddies and I planned to duplicate the Potawatomi crossing."

"Didja?" Ross had asked.

Michael replied. "Almost. But not quite."

Anne broke in with, "Don't talk about that, Mike. It could give them ideas."

But Brendon's dad continued anyway.

On a warm, sunny afternoon one guy took a late ferry to the mainland. His job was to find a spot for the signal fire, then start it after sundown. Back on the island, the rest of them "borrowed" two canoes from a resort on West Harbor, paddled to the edge of the bay, and watched for the fire.

Finally, about midnight, they convinced themselves they saw it. Of course, there were so many lights on the mainland that no signal fire would have stood out. "But that was a minor point," Michael had said. "We *believed* we saw it so we took off, paddling like crazy. We just didn't get very far."

As soon as they had cleared the island, they'd gotten caught in a steady northwest wind that turned out to be far stronger than they were. They swamped the canoes, lost their paddles in the dark, and then drifted helplessly until the

17

current washed them up on Plum Island. They had stumbled up the beach, cold and wet and scared, and banged on the Coast Guard station door.

"The commander took one look at us and said we were either real crazy or real stupid or both," Michael told them. "But what I really was, was very lucky."

"Did you practice with the canoes?" Brendon had asked. "You know, train for it?"

"*Train* for it!" Michael had said, laughing. "If we'd have *trained* for it, we would've seen how dangerous it was and stayed home."

But Brendon knew that his father prized the experience. Again Michael had tested fate, scared himself witless just for fun. And that was the point—Michael did dangerous things for the pure enjoyment of beating desperate odds.

And sometimes Brendon hated him for it.

• • •

At last they were directed onto the ferry. Brendon noticed the observation deck was already crowded with boisterous sightseers defying the chilly wind and threat of rain.

"I think I'm staying in the car," Anne said. "You guys can get out and look around if you want."

"How 'bout it?" Ross asked Brendon.

"No thanks."

"Okay," said Ross, opening his door. "Be right back." He climbed out, pushed the door shut, and hurried over to the metal staircase leading up to the pilot house.

Abruptly, two blasts from the boat's big horn startled Anne and Brendon. They jerked forward, hunching their shoulders, and laughed nervously.

"We're off," Anne said, as the rumbling diesel engines sent

18

the fully loaded ferry into the pitching, wind-whipped waters.

It wasn't long before the bow began to take on the breakers. One mammoth wave jarred the boat and sent a shower of spray over all the cars parked in the first three rows.

Suddenly, Ross was at the door, bracing himself against an adjacent car.

"*Sheeesh!*" he said as he crawled in and pulled the door closed. "What a mess."

"I agree," said Anne.

They rode the waves in silence for the next fifteen minutes.

When the wind died down a little, Anne tilted her seat back, reclined, and said, "Could you guys stay quiet and let me doze? I'm suddenly very tired."

"Sure," said Brendon.

"Join you," said Ross.

After the boat cleared the island's western tip, the big swells vanished. Soon even Brendon was on the verge of sleep . . . soothing sleep . . . almost there, in fact . . . crossing to the calm, quiet realm, when his mother—

SCREAMED!!

Brendon shot up to a straight-backed position and saw his mother gripping the steering wheel, her eyes wide open.

"Wha'?" muttered Ross from the back seat.

"What's with you!" flared Brendon.

Anne leaned forward, burying her face in her hands, her forehead against the top edge of the steering wheel, trying to laugh at herself but not succeeding. "I thought I'd fallen asleep at the wheel. I must have been dreaming. I forgot where we were. I saw myself—"

"Hey, relax," interrupted Brendon.

"I'm sorry."

"That's okay," said Ross.

The three of them then watched silently as the captain brought the boat into Detroit Harbor and up to the dock. Under cloudy skies, vacation had started.

5

Getting the car off the ferry was simpler than boarding. In only a few minutes Brendon and his mother and brother were pulling away from the landing, following the red-inked route line Grampa Carl had drawn on the map.

They were to take Lobdell Point Road north until it began bending east and intersected with West Harbor Road. There they would turn, go half a mile on West Harbor, and start looking for an oversized blue mailbox with the name "A. Hawkins" printed in white block letters. Next to the box would be a gravel driveway leading down to Dr. Arthur Hawkins's summer home.

They'd found West Harbor Road and were moving slowly along the winding pavement, glimpsing the water through thick stands of birch, maple, hemlock, and cedar. They felt reverent as they drove beneath the cathedral-arched trees lining the roadway.

Suddenly the spell was broken. An impatient cycle rider revved up behind them, screeching his horn. After two long blasts, he popped his clutch and roared past them, glowering at Anne and swearing at her.

"Go get him!" said Ross. "Ten bucks a hit!"

"Ross!" said Anne, irritated.

Ross added, "The guy's ejaculating right now, I'll bet anything."

"*Ross!*" Anne yelled angrily. "Stop it!"

Brendon offered a smile that was ragged at the edges. This was not something he would endure, jerks and creeps. He wouldn't forget the red "33" stamped on the back of the cyclist's silver fishnet football jersey. Brendon listened carefully and heard the staccato of the cycle engine go quickly faint when the rider disappeared around the next turn.

As they reached the turn, Brendon was surprised to see the cyclist again. He had pulled onto the shoulder, his bike idling as he straddled it. His attention was directed toward a very pretty blond girl in white shorts, who'd been walking.

Brendon edged closer to the window. He wanted a good look at both of them. Just as they neared the couple, as Brendon was getting another view of the guy's face, Ross reached over Anne's shoulder and blared the horn.

"Ross!" Anne yelled again, as the cyclist jumped and nearly lost his balance, nearly toppled his bike. The girl laughed, covering her mouth. While the cyclist scowled at them, Brendon's eyes met the girl's. She lifted her brows a fraction. Then, as the car rolled past, she smiled at Brendon from behind the cyclist and shook her head slightly. Brendon smiled back before Anne coasted into the next turn.

"Ross, why did you do that?" scolded Anne. "We haven't been here five minutes and you're already in trouble."

"Chopperhead's got the trouble," said Ross. "I've got Big Brother to protect me, remember?"

"Yeah, right," said Brendon.

"So you *deal* with him, Bro," Ross ordered, waving in the cyclist's direction.

"Whatever's necessary," said Brendon, meaning it.

"Oh, stop that now, you two," Anne cut in. "This is Washington Island, not Dodge City, the Wild West."

"Uh-huh," said Ross. "A double TV allusion there. Good show, Mom."

Before Anne could reply, Ross spotted the blue mailbox. Anne turned in the driveway and followed the curving gravel road down to the nearly hidden single-story redwood structure. The clapboards had been freshly stained. The sandy beach not fifty feet from the cottage was being pounded by wave after wave. A stiff wind came straight at them from the west.

"I wonder who did that?" said Anne, gesturing at the staining.

"Why?" asked Brendon.

"Because Dr. Hawkins seldom comes up here anymore. He rents the place to friends most of the summer. Supposedly, he's thinking of selling it."

"Is that why Grampa wanted us to take it?" asked Ross. "He's going to make a bid?"

"I never thought of that," said Anne. "I'll check when I call him, after we're settled in."

They parked behind the cottage and walked around to the north side, where they found an entrance. Anne unlocked the thick wooden door. Inside, everything was spotless. They stood in a little kitchen and looked west out of a huge picture window. They watched the black and purple clouds hang over the churning water in the bay.

Between them and the window was a dark oak dining room set with four high-back chairs. Nearby were a matching leather sofa and chair, set at angles so they faced the water and the massive fieldstone fireplace on the far half of the north wall. The walls were covered with knotty pine tongue-

and-groove paneling, and colorful braided rugs lay on the gleaming hardwood floors.

The three bedrooms covered the entire south wall of the cottage. The bathroom had been newly remodeled.

"Nice," said Ross.

"Yes," replied Anne.

"Give me the trunk key, and I'll start unpacking," said Ross.

Anne held out the key and said, "Brendon, it's chilly in here. Could you start a fire?"

"Sure." Brendon moved closer to the fireplace and spotted the wood box in the shadows. It was full of dry oak and birch logs and even contained newspapers and kindling. "Somebody thought of everything," he said.

"I hope so," Anne sighed. "I'm really exhausted. What time is it?"

"A little past five," said Ross, lugging in a pair of suitcases.

"Okay," she said, holding her fingertips to her temples, thinking. "You two unpack while I look over the kitchen. When the car is empty I'll run out for some groceries. Is there anything you'd especially like for supper?"

"Anything'll do fine," Brendon said.

"And plenty of it," said Ross.

• • •

After supper, they sat reading in front of the soothing fire. Outside, the storm that had been organizing itself all day finally struck. As the wind surged, the cottage creaked. For a few moments they could barely hear over the rain drumming the roof. One barrage of thunder rattled the windows and made everyone look up at the same time.

Eventually, the rain became a steady wash, and they were reading comfortably again. Anne perused the Milwaukee

24

newspaper she'd picked up at Mann's Store, while Ross squinted with intensity at an old *Sports Illustrated* article about the NBA playoffs. Brendon studied the little twenty-page *Door Lore* booklet he'd picked from a rack at the North-port ferry dock. In the pamphlet he found the Porte des Morts story his father had told him, plus some new facts. They wouldn't be changing the name soon, he thought, as he read:

> Since the Potawatomi-Winnebago tragedy, many more people have died trying to pass through Death's Door. LaSalle's ship *The Griffin* left Detroit Harbor in 1679 and was never seen again. According to the diary of a Plum Island lighthouse keeper, nearly a hundred ships were damaged or sunk while crossing the strait in 1871. From 1872 to 1889, shipwrecks occurred at least twice a week.
>
> Even in the twentieth century, Death's Door has lived up to its reputation. On November 7, 1914, the schooner *Resumption* grounded itself on Plum Island after battling the rough seas of Porte des Morts. The ship finally broke up and joined over two hundred other sunken vessels—enough to support a growing scuba diving industry.
>
> And nearly every summer since, an occasional tourist family (or even a native) drowns there when the wild currents, which sometimes flow against the wind, capsize small boats.

Nice place, thought Brendon.

6

Sunday was clear and bright.

The boys slept in.

When they awakened, they discovered their mother was missing. Ross found the note. It said she had gone out for some breakfast rolls and a newspaper, and told them to hold down the fort. Ross pocketed the message before Brendon ever saw it.

When Anne finally returned, Brendon said, "See, I told you," to Ross.

"What's that?" Ross answered, reading his *Sports Illustrated*.

Anne glanced at Brendon's irritated expression, then at Ross's mocking one.

"What did he tell you?" Anne asked Brendon. Her eyes narrowed with suspicion.

"That you deserted us here for some kind of Outward Bound thing, a survival test."

"You *didn't*," said Anne, looking accusingly at Ross.

Ross shrugged and eyed Brendon as though he were crazy.

"He said it," Brendon replied coolly.

"I didn't say she 'deserted' us. I said she 'deserved' us, coupla champs, you know?"

"Ahhhh, the punchline," said Brendon. Then after a pause, "Sometimes you're just not very funny."

The mood suddenly darkened, seemed dangerous. Ross frowned.

"Here," Anne said, cutting off the confrontation. "You guys have some breakfast and try to get along. There's a Sunday paper too, if you're interested."

Ross was interested in the sports section. Brendon continued to plow through a booklet on the topography of Washington Island.

A short time later Ross asked, "Wanna go biking a little this afternoon?"

"Maybe," Brendon said, looking up. "Maybe not."

"Mom?"

"I don't think so. I'm going to stay here and be lazy."

"You deserve it," said Ross. Then to his brother, "Brendon, c'mon. You need a little action."

Brendon shrugged but gave Ross the nod.

• • •

Ross led Brendon up West Harbor Road. They had planned to stay on the paved roads this trip, so they would be able to explore only the western half of the island.

Brendon clipped along on his ten-speed, enjoying the washed air and the hypnotic pumping of the pedals. The boys saw no other bicyclists until they reached Main Road. There they turned due north and passed through uptown Washington Island, the *commercial* zone. A few restaurants and stores seemed to be doing most of the island business. They also met the first of the moped-mounted day trippers who'd arrived on the ferry that morning.

Quickly Brendon and Ross left uptown and continued riding north. They crossed the island on Jackson Harbor Road, then went south to Sand Dunes park. At the Dunes they just walked their bikes in to check out the view, since the area was already crowded.

Instead of swimming, they took South Shore Drive west, passing a big marina and several small, old-fashioned resort hotels. By staying along the shore, they arrived back at Main Road. They ended their trip by visiting the Island School and Community Center.

There they were surprised to find a group of high school guys playing pick-up basketball on a well-maintained asphalt court behind the buildings. Ross glanced at Brendon with an expectant look.

"Wanna join 'em?" Ross asked.

"Not today. You go ahead."

"What'll you do, watch?"

"Not this time."

"Then what?"

"Go home and rest. Maybe swim. Don't worry about it."

"You sure it's okay?"

"Oh, I'll miss you something terrible, of course. But I'll manage," Brendon replied, deadpan.

"See ya," said Ross as he pedaled over to the game.

When Ross stepped onto the court and made the first shot he attempted, his form flawless (as it always would be, after the hours of drilling Michael had put him through), Brendon pulled out of the school yard and headed south on Main Road. His brother's amazing basketball skill was the obvious result of a closeness with Michael that Brendon hadn't enjoyed, so every shot Ross made reminded Brendon of what he'd somehow missed.

He pedaled off and hooked around to West Harbor Road,

returning to the cottage by the same route they'd driven yesterday.

As he hummed along the bike path on his way to West Harbor Road, he noticed a lot more tourist traffic. Mopeds and bicycles wobbled everywhere. Nearly every passing car had an out-of-state license plate. Brendon even saw a couple of tour trains pulling visitors around the island in little canvas-roofed cars towed by red trucks.

Brendon pedaled on, lost in thought, not noticing for a few moments the white hardtop Jeep CJ that had slowed to keep pace with him. When it finally caught his attention, he looked over and saw a girl driving and leaning toward him, checking him out. The girl from yesterday. He smiled cautiously. She waved, then accelerated.

Must be the weather, thought Brendon. The lake effect. Summer.

Though he didn't see that much of her, he saw enough. Her curly blond hair flowed to her shoulders. Her tall, slender, athletic figure looked smooth and tan. She was beautiful.

Brendon felt good all the way back to the cottage.

· · ·

As he came down the curving driveway, he saw the car was gone. Inside, on the kitchen counter, he found a note from Anne. She had driven over to Sievers School on the northeast side of the island. She wanted to explore the facility before beginning her class on Monday.

Brendon decided to take a book down to the beach, open up a chaise lounge, lie back, and get some sun. Shirtless, in faded maroon gym shorts, Brendon tried to read a Travis McGee mystery but couldn't stay with it. Soon the sun, soft breeze, and hypnotic surging of the waves made him drowsy. He laid the book aside and dozed off.

• • •

"He was there," said Ross.

"Wha'?" muttered Brendon, waking. "What? What time is it?"

"Four o'clock," Ross answered. "He was there."

"Who?" asked Brendon, irritated.

"Chopperhead. The screamer from yesterday."

"Where?" Brendon was suddenly wide awake, pushing himself up on one elbow, shading his eyes in the bright glare.

"At the game. He showed up maybe ten minutes after you left. He came with another guy. And he's real intense."

"What's his name?" Brendon was trying to sound bored.

"Clayton, I think."

"*Clayton?* Who names anybody Clayton?"

"Clayton's dada, I imagine."

"Hm."

"Where's Mom?"

"At the weaving school, scouting the place."

"You been sleeping the whole time?"

"Pretty much."

"Well, get with it."

"Meaning?"

"This is vacation. Try to live it up."

Brendon stared at his brother for a three-count, then said, "Don't get on me."

"Fishing."

". . . Pardon?"

"A guy from the game, an islander, told me there's a good place for bass and perch just around the point there." Ross waved toward the south edge of the harbor.

"There's only one oar in the boat. I looked."

"Take the canoe."

"Fish from a canoe?"

"Back to nature. Primitive and original."

"Original," Brendon repeated, picking himself up from the lounge, standing and stretching, then following Ross over to the utility shed to get the rods.

• • •

Minutes later they had paddled around the point and entered the next bay south of them, Figenschau Bay. The boys steered the canoe along the bay's northeastern rim, looking for a good place to cast. Brendon scanned the woods, noting the well-maintained and widely spaced summer homes. It wasn't until they were halfway down the eastern shore that he saw her.

She was wearing white cotton running shorts, a blue-and-white striped jersey, and tennis shoes. She had her back to them, stooping and looking at something hidden in the brush near a log cabin. Behind a corner of the building Brendon spotted the front fender and wheel of her white Jeep. Mouth agape, he stopped paddling.

"What have we here?" he heard Ross whisper. "Stalking the wildwood nymph, huh?" Then, doing his uncanny Marlin Perkins/*Wild Kingdom* impersonation, Ross continued, "While I wait in the blind, Brendon will hold the net and attempt to bag this elusive beauty."

"Shhhhh," urged Brendon, still staring.

The boys floated in place, watching as the blond girl struggled to pull what looked like an old wooden skiff through some scraggly bushes. She wasn't having much luck. Her tightly muscled legs and shoulders strained.

"Need some help?" Brendon called out.

"Oh no," said Marlin Perkins again, "I believe Brendon has blown our cover. We'll have to move fast now if we hope to corner our prey."

The girl turned to face them, squinting across the thirty yards of water between herself and the canoe. She smiled.

"No thanks," she yelled back, her voice clear and clean. "I can manage."

Brendon was about to ask, "You sure?" when Marlin murmured, "Well, bad luck. It looks like we've lost her for today. Brendon has aroused the guardian of the lair."

Brendon looked at Ross, followed his line of vision to the cabin porch, and spotted a tall, stocky, neatly bearded man wearing a plain white polo shirt and khaki shorts. The man stared skeptically but not meanly at them. He folded his arms across his barrel chest. He did not speak. He looked back at the girl.

"It's okay, Dad. He just offered to help." She was talking quietly, but her words floated across the water and reached the canoe.

Still silent, the father brought his disturbing gaze back to the boys.

"Well . . . bye now," said Brendon, trying to sound both courteous and confident. He started to paddle frantically.

"We can only wonder," said Marlin, "why young Brendon didn't tell them 'Have a nice day' too."

"Shut up," Brendon suggested, digging hard with his paddle.

Ross wasn't helping.

"C'mon," groaned Brendon. "Gimme a break."

With their strokes synchronized now, the boys moved swiftly to the far south side of the bay.

"You know her from somewhere?" Ross asked in his normal voice.

"I'm not sure. I think she's the girl we saw yesterday. The one you honked at."

"Oh yeahhhh. You're right."

"And she waved to me this afternoon."

"Holy moley," said Ross, The Nerd. "I didn't realize you were *involved*."

Brendon rolled his eyes and shook his head.

"I bet she's worth it, though," said Ross.

"Worth what?"

"Making a geek of yourself in front of her old man just to hear her talk."

"One of your faults is you don't understand risk-takers."

"Risk-taker? You?"

"Watch me."

"Always, Bro," said Ross. "Always." Then, as Marlin Perkins, Ross added, "Brendon can take these big risks . . . but the rest of us don't have to. With Mutual of Omaha—"

"Drop it!" snapped Brendon.

7

The Turners drifted quietly through the week. Anne enjoyed her first sessions of Beginning Weaving. She told Brendon how calming and peaceful the day-long classes were. "But the time goes by very quickly," she pointed out, "because everyone is so *involved*, so committed to learning and improving technique. Weaving is a wonderful ritual, it really is. You know we have people there from all over the country?"

Anne was also particularly pleased to learn one of the school's administrative assistants was an old friend. Beth Kelly, now Beth Neal, was a native islander who'd waitressed with Anne the summer she met Michael. After becoming reacquainted and hearing of Michael's accident, Beth called two other women Anne had known. The four were to meet on Saturday, play golf perhaps.

Ross continued to be his well-adjusted self. He'd already become a fixture on the playground basketball court and been invited to the homes of several other players.

Brendon was another case. He'd spent most of his time either alone at the cottage or with Ross at the cottage.

He'd been reading a lot, especially material on the island. He wanted to care about where he was, but he was having trouble finding something attractive enough to bring him out. Basketball wouldn't do it. Nor would fishing or swimming or biking.

Occasionally he thought about the blond girl. He knew he wanted to meet her, but not just yet. Besides, he could be wrong about her. She might not be worth the risk.

Late Thursday afternoon of their first week, as the boys finished supper and Ross was leaving to meet one of his basketball pals, Anne said, "Is there anything going on tonight? Anything fun you *both* could do?"

"Might hit the Barn," said Ross between his last gulps of Seven-Up.

"The Red Barn? It's still in business?" she said, amazed.

"Uh-huh. There's hot rockin'."

"What?" said Brendon, looking up from his island map.

"Thursdays," Ross said. "They have live bands. Dances."

"Live bands? Where'd they find any?"

"Got me. Tonight's supposed to be good, though."

"Why?"

"It's this group called Change-Up. They've sort of been vacationing here, a place on the east side. They're writing some songs. They've made albums."

"Yeah? Change-Up, huh. Never heard of 'em."

"I guess they're pretty big in Chicago. At least that's what *Clayton* says."

"And of course Clayton knows everything that happens in Chicago," said Brendon.

"Absolutely," answered Ross.

"Who's Clayton?" asked Anne.

"Just a guy from the playground," Ross replied. He glanced at his watch and said, "Gotta run. A most pleasant repast, Mother." He bowed gallantly.

35

Anne made a face and watched Ross as he cleared his dishes and then hurried out the door.

With Ross gone, the meal continued in silence. Finally, Anne said, "Do you like it here?"

"Ummm."

"Brendon?"

"Sure," he said, meeting her gaze. "Why?"

"I mean, are you getting along okay?"

"You're worried about me, too much the loner."

Anne put on a look of concern.

"Don't worry," Brendon said. "I'm doing just what I want. So let's drop it, okay?"

"But I still worry."

"I know."

"Being alone all day isn't good. That's a fact, not just opinion."

"Objective medical advice."

"Yes. I'm serious."

"Well, don't be. When it's time to worry, you'll know."

"What does that mean?"

Brendon shrugged. "Got me," he said.

Anne sighed, looked out the picture window. "We talked about spending time here every year," she said softly, "but something always came up."

"*Always.*"

Once again there was a strained silence.

"Brendon?"

"Yeah?"

"Promise me something."

"Sure. What?"

"That you'll give this place a chance."

Brendon looked down, thought a moment, then asked,

"How can I convince you I'm not crazy?"

"I guess I'm concerned because you want to be alone so much. I know it's none of my business after a certain point. I know we're all different people. It's just that—"

"You think I should go mix and match at the Red Barn tonight," Brendon cut in, aiming his index finger at his mother. "Is that it?" He was teasing her a little and she knew it. "You want me to be normal, red-blooded."

"Well, not necessarily that, but maybe . . ."

"Maybe what?"

"You could go for a while just to see what it's like."

"Be a party hopper?"

"Meet some new people."

"Why?"

"To get outside yourself more."

"And then what?"

"You can't hide forever, Brendon."

"Why not? And who says I'm hiding?"

"What are you doing?"

"Thinking, looking, planning."

"Planning what?" Anne's voice sounded suddenly strained.

"I don't know."

"Brendon . . ."

He looked closely at his mother's face and saw real fear.

"Brendon, did you hear me?"

Brendon saw the fear again, but said nothing.

"You wouldn't ever . . . hurt yourself, would you?" she asked.

"Huh?" For a moment Brendon had no idea what his mother was driving at. Then it hit him. "*Kill* myself?" he asked in shock. "Is that what you're saying?"

Anne gave him a quick nod, her lips compressed.

"Not if I can help it," he said calmly.

"Promise me you'll never, *ever*—"

"Please don't *worry*," Brendon replied, touching his mother's arm. "Look, if it'll make you feel better, I'll go out tonight, okay?" Already he was thinking of what he could do if the Red Barn party looked too complicated. He might take a long walk or a bike ride.

"You don't have to go, really," said Anne, pulling Brendon back to the conversation.

"Sure I do," he said. "I've got something to prove."

"What?"

"I'm normal."

8

Dressed in a light blue knit shirt, tan poplin slacks, and topsiders, Brendon climbed on his bike and began his ride to South Shore Drive and toward the Red Barn. Already the sky was mauve where the sun was going down.

Pedaling easily, he knew he could just ride off in the night. He didn't have to go there and be with people, strangers.

Yet he somehow felt drawn to the challenge, this boy-girl scene. It looked like the hard thing, a dangerous thing. It could end in disaster. It could be The Brink. But that appealed to him tonight. He had no idea why.

It was dark by the time he arrived at the Barn. The air was still balmy and clean, the night fresh and inviting. He hid his bike, chaining it to a tree in a little stand of birch located well away from the building. As for the Red Barn, it was just that, an old barn. Brendon could see it had been recently painted. And somebody had done a good job of surfacing a large patio area behind it. Brendon saw dancers there who'd spilled outdoors.

Brendon entered through a side door. By then the band was taking a break. Brendon scanned the crowd in the dimly lit hall, searching for his brother. He couldn't find him. He recognized no one. As he moved cautiously around clusters of five and six, he felt tense and self-conscious. The faces he saw were friendly, though. Girls even smiled at him. And he tried to smile back, but he knew he was faking and thought everybody could tell. He realized how scared he was. Maybe he could just cut through the place once and be done.

He was close to the other exit when the band returned. He stopped a moment to watch them. At least, he thought, they looked professional and had lots of new equipment. And when they struck the first chord of their next song, Brendon knew Change-Up was for real, a team of musicians. Soon they were doing tight four-part backup harmony.

Brendon was leaning against a thick wall-beam, enjoying the sounds, when she entered through the same door he'd used. He was surprised but not too surprised. This was where she'd be, a girl with her looks.

She made her way across the crowded dance floor, glancing around at first, but then showing a whimsical half-smile when she saw him. She wore a lightweight boat-neck sweater, white cords, and sandals. Her clothes set off her flawless, tanned face and blond curls. Brendon's heart slowed to long, throbbing beats. He swallowed hard as panic hit. She had nearly reached him now. He was struggling to form an opening line when she was intercepted.

From nowhere, broad-backed Clayton—his dark hair slicked, his black nylon muscle shirt sculpted to his body— stepped between them. Brendon slowly leaned back again and tried to calm down. Clayton hadn't noticed him.

"Hi, gorgeous!" Clayton said loudly. "Remember me?" He reached out and rested a hand on her shoulder. She stiffened but didn't stop him. She said nothing, just looked at him vacantly.

"So, wanna dance?" he asked as the band ended its song.

She responded by batting her eyes a little. Then she tilted her head and replied in an irritating, breathy whine, "Well, you know, this is unreal, but like this next dance is like already taken, you know?"

Boy-oh-boy, thought Brendon, looking to bolt now.

"Huh?" said Clayton, removing his hand from her shoulder, letting it fall to his side.

She showed her sparkling white teeth and shrugged.

"Let's start over," said Clayton gamely. "Me, I'm Clay Wills, and I wanna know you, okay? All right so far? So I've seen you around. I think we might have a lot in common."

That line started her giggling.

"What's funny?" he asked.

"*Clay*," she said, still snickering.

"What about it?"

"Like, once there was this boy we called Clay, in my ceramics class?"

"So?"

"Well, I mean, like you know, Clay wasn't his actual name?"

"That's really fascinating," remarked Wills, nodding sagely. "Wanna step outside, tell me more?"

To his surprise, Brendon felt sorry for Clay, being charmed by this bimbo.

"I'm so sure!" the girl replied. "Like I just *got here*, you know? So anyway, we called him that cuz he kept wiping his hands, you know, on his pants? Whenever he was throwing a pot?"

"Yeah?" said Clay, with a nervous laugh.

"Well, like I don't mean just *anywhere* on his pants, you know? Like it was always in . . . embarrassing places?"

"No lie."

"No. So like he was always *full of it* . . . clay, I mean." She laughed in his face, covering her mouth with her long, slender fingers, her eyes watching for his reaction. Then she caught Brendon's attention and winked at him.

Clayton took a step back, gave her a measuring look. He decided to try once more. "How 'bout a ride?" he asked. Clayton extended his arms, made fists with his hands and flicked his wrists like he was revving his cycle. Brendon expected him to say, "Varoom-varoooom!" next. But Clay tried, "There's a big party goin' down near my place."

"Uh-uh. No can do," she said, still in that irritating small voice.

"Look, we're talkin' run of the house, a big pontoon boat for midnight cruisin', all sorts of joy stuff. Get tight and act loose, okay?"

"Joy stuff?"

Finally, Clayton shook his head, looked to the side. Then facing her again he said, "Baby, when you return to planet Earth, let me know. I still think we should get together."

"Un-REAL," she said as he marched off, shouldering his way through the dancers and disappearing out the door. By then the band had resumed playing.

Brendon turned to the girl and found her staring at him, smiling guardedly. She looked like somebody he knew and he wanted to say so, but it would sound dumb, like he was making it up. So instead he offered, "That's not your real voice . . . is it?"

"Like, how can you be so sure?" she replied.

Brendon was stuck. He might have gone for the door himself if she hadn't said, "You know that guy?" She tilted her head in the direction Clay had disappeared.

42

"Not really."

"Well, his father's some hot-shot developer." The airhead voice was gone. "I hear he wants to turn this place into one big shopping mall."

"The island?"

"Right."

"Enclosed?"

"Probably," she said, laughing.

"You know a lot about him."

"Enough."

"But he doesn't know you know it?"

"Uh-uh."

"That's when knowing is fun, I suppose."

"Yeah," she said, staring directly into his eyes, smiling warmly now. "I'm Courtney Holmes."

"Brendon Turner."

"Where're you from?"

"Minneapolis. You?"

"Chicago. Ever been there?"

He shook his head. A silence built.

"Like, you know . . . wanna dance?"

Without speaking, hearing that Change-Up was doing a slow, dreamy one, he reached for her hand, encircling her back with his other arm. He couldn't believe himself, how relaxed he felt. He hadn't been with a girl this way since his breakup with Lisa Young.

"Do I know you," Courtney asked matter-of-factly, "or do you know me?"

"You look familiar."

"My father says when you get old enough, everyone looks familiar."

43

Brendon smiled.

"My father's Philip Holmes," she continued. "Heard of him?"

"Should I?"

"Well, he's a writer, a novelist, and his book is selling. He's getting famous around here."

"What's the title?"

"*Door Bluff*. It's a mystery."

"I don't know it."

They continued to shuffle along until Brendon asked, "You get your boat in the water?"

"Too heavy. It's wood and been sitting there all spring."

"Will it float?"

"That's what I wanted to find out. Philip says I'm old enough now to be responsible for his *baby*."

"He kidding?"

"I don't know. I never know."

"You call him Philip."

"Ever since he left."

Brendon stared back, confused.

"Divorce," she said. "Last year."

"Oh." Then, desperate for a topic, Brendon asked, "You gonna try taking the boat out again?"

"Absolutely."

"I'll help." Brendon had said it before he could catch himself. He'd stopped concentrating for a moment and bang, he'd gotten into something. "I mean, if you need me," he added.

She lifted her head to look him in the eye. "Maybe we do," she said as the song ended. They danced together for another two songs before she said, "Like, you know, I gotta run. This was just a little sneak-and-peek mission." She glanced at her watch.

"Busy schedule," said Brendon.

"I have to be up early."

Brendon smiled, looked at the floor.

"C'mon," she said and started moving toward the exit. Brendon followed. Just before walking out, she asked, "You need a ride someplace? I think we're going the same way. West side?"

"Thanks, but Mom gave me the Schwinn tonight."

She squinted at him skeptically. "No joke?"

"No joke."

"What next," she commented, her tone ambiguous.

"I'll walk you to your Jeep," he offered.

"That'd be nice."

When they left the Barn, they ran right into Clay. He was straddling his big black cycle, talking to a couple of buddies. As Courtney and Brendon passed by, Clayton and his friends fell silent. Clay glowered at Brendon. Brendon slowed, looked back directly at him.

Finally, after several long moments, Clay gave up. He looked off and mumbled something to his pals. They nodded glumly. Brendon took Courtney's elbow and led her away.

Her Jeep was parked on the edge of the gravel drive down where it joined South Shore. Again, Brendon felt his confidence fading. He searched for something to talk about. How had he gotten caught up in all this scene?

Finally, he opted for, "That boat looks pretty old." What a lame comment, he thought.

"Like I said, it's Philip's." They were standing next to her Jeep now, facing each other, Brendon with his back to the gravel driveway. "He built it when he was young," explained Courtney.

"He lives up here."

"Now he does."

"How long?"

"Since fall. After the divorce."

"Oh."

"When he was a kid he spent summers here. My grandparents had a place."

"Still?"

"No. They're both dead."

"Were they very old?" Brendon asked, calculating likely ages.

"No. It was cancer."

"Both?"

"Uh-huh. Pretty depressing, right?"

"Did you get to know them?"

"Sure. They died just the year before last."

Brendon thought briefly about Michael, but pushed him out of his mind by asking, "Where'd your dad keep the boat? It wasn't outside all that time."

"Somebody's barn. I don't know who."

Brendon nodded. He felt painfully inept and searched for a graceful way to pull out of the conversation.

"He built it himself for the Channel Challenge," she continued. "Ever heard of that? They're bringing it back."

"Where'd it go?" Brendon asked. "What is it?"

"A small-boat race, sailboats only, to the island and back."

"Back to what? Not the mainland."

"No. From Washington Island to Rock Island, two laps."

"That's better," said Brendon. "Safer anyway." He'd read about Rock Island. The place stood maybe a mile off Washington Island's northeast coast and was now entirely a state park, no private lands, no cars. "What'd you mean 'They're bringing it back'?" he wondered.

"The race was traditional during the Fourth of July celebration. They dropped it a long time ago because a little boy got killed."

"How?"

"Fell out of a boat and was hit by the next one. He drowned before they could get to him."

Brendon stared at Courtney. "Why bring it back now?"

"People want it. There's interest. And no one in the boy's family lives here anymore."

"So you're going to race?"

"With Philip, I guess. It's his thing. If we can get the boat in shape," she added. "That's why I have to be up early tomorrow."

"Maintenance detail."

"The pits."

Brendon glanced over to where his bike was parked.

"Know what?" she asked, calling him back.

He shook his head.

"I haven't asked anything about you?"

"There's not much to tell," Brendon said. He raised his guard.

"Why are you here?"

"To get away from it all," he answered.

"From what?"

Brendon had had enough by now. It was definitely time to disappear. She was getting too close. Then suddenly they were *there*: she asked, "You with the family, Mom and Dad?"

"Mom and brother."

"No Dad?"

Brendon swallowed hard, then managed to get it out. "He died last February in a car accident."

A terrible silence formed before Courtney broke it. "I'm sorry," she said. "Really. I shouldn't be so nosy. It's just that—"

Her words were cut by the roar of Clayton's motorcycle. He barreled at them from the shadows up the driveway, flashing on his headlamp. The fishtailing, cleated rear tire kicked gravel and dirt against the backs of Brendon's legs, wrecking his pants.

"Dammit!" growled Brendon, glaring at Wills, wanting to give chase, but having to watch helplessly as the cycle disappeared into the night. He looked down at the mess.

"Sorry," said Brendon, referring to his language.

"*He's* got the decorum problem," said Courtney.

"Huh?"

"Boy's got no manners."

"Something else he won't have," said Brendon, his face hot with humiliation.

"Forget him."

Brendon bent down, tried to brush off some of the grit.

"He's a creep," said Courtney, "and a little scary. That's my opinion after only a week."

"Yeah," said Brendon, looking at her now.

"Listen, let me drive you home, okay?"

"What about the Schwinn?"

"Throw it in back. Where is it?"

"Over there," said Brendon, pointing to the clump of birch. In the moonlight the trees looked like pale bones.

They climbed into the Jeep and rode down to where the bike was still securely chained. Brendon freed it and lifted it

48

into the Jeep. Then Courtney jounced the CJ onto South Shore Drive.

"Where to?" she asked.

"West Harbor Road," he answered, inspecting his ruined pants again.

"Don't waste any more time on him, okay? He's a goof."

Brendon didn't reply, and the silence lengthened. His mind began to drift.

Courtney brought him back abruptly with, "You and your dad, were you pretty close?" Courtney stared straight ahead, then sneaked a glance at him, which he caught.

"Sometimes," said Brendon, startled and self-conscious. "Good as it gets, I'm afraid."

Another pause elapsed before Courtney said, "I don't know Philip very well at all, not the revised version anyway. He surprises me."

"The revised version," repeated Brendon.

"He's an alkie," she said. "Recovering."

"Since when?"

"Since a while after they split. Almost a year."

"Oh."

"He's up here trying to put it together, stay clean, make it right, all that."

"Have you seen him much? Since he left, I mean."

"Not like this, being here."

"How'd he write a book?" Brendon wondered.

"Being a drunk?"

"Yeah."

"Lots of drunks write books," she said. But then she saved Brendon further embarrassment by adding, "Only Philip *couldn't* write his books, and that's why he drank."

"I don't get it."

"He wanted to write novels full-time, but we couldn't afford it. So he wrote ad copy and hated that and made way too much money and hung around way too many office parties and conventions and got drunk all the time and ruined everything for us. But he got his book, didn't he?"

Her sarcasm upset Brendon. "So it's a little strained," he commented.

"Not this week. He's really different, very open and honest. I like him so far."

"That's good."

"I hope it lasts."

By now they were nearing the Hawkins place and Brendon pointed out the blue mailbox. "Here," he said.

"Hawkins?"

"Friend of the family."

"Uh-huh."

"Well . . . thanks." Brendon smiled and started to climb out, relaxed but glad the night was ending.

"I wasn't kidding about tomorrow," blurted Courtney. "Working on the boat."

"Shouldn't you check with your dad first?"

"Yeah, I suppose. If he says it's okay?"

"I don't know. It seems like a pretty personal thing."

"I'm still going to check."

"Why?"

Instead of answering, Courtney asked, "Know what?"

Brendon shook his head.

"I can't believe how much we've told each other."

"I haven't said much," Brendon replied defensively.

"More than you think."

Brendon looked down. "I'll get my bike," he said.

"So maybe I'll see you tomorrow?"

Brendon lifted out the Schwinn and said, "Anything's possible."

He glanced up at her, their eyes met, held. And he smiled.

9

The next morning Brendon slept in. Or pretended to. He could hear his mother and brother having an early breakfast, planning their busy days. Anne sounded excited about Sievers, and Ross had been invited fishing by one of the ballplayers from the school yard. The two times his mother peeked in to check on Brendon, he faked deep sleep. She didn't try to wake him.

Brendon had lots of reasons for hiding out. He didn't want to face his mother's Did-you-have-fun-last-night cross-examination. And he certainly wasn't ready for any of Ross's wisecracking. Who knows what *he* saw, heard from the guys. Wills would start bragging up his strafe job on Brendon right away, he was sure of it. And even though he liked her, enjoyed talking to her last night, Courtney too threatened his peace of mind. Brendon wanted no complications, not now.

When he heard the door being closed and locked, followed by the slap-whack of the screen door, Brendon knew he was safe, for a while anyway. He lay there, listening carefully to make sure he was alone. After several minutes of hearing only the chirping of birds and muffled splashes of breaking waves, Brendon slid out of bed.

52

He stood up, stretched, shuffled to the door, pulled it open, and heard—

"Who is she?"

Brendon stopped dead, surprised but trying not to show it. There sat Ross, wearing a smug little smile, telling Brendon he'd fooled himself more than his younger brother.

"Thought you were gone," Brendon mumbled, heading for the bathroom.

"You hardly ever sleep this late," said Ross. "And I'd hang around no matter how long it took."

"What took?"

"Get you to spill."

"You were there."

"Oh sure."

"I didn't see you."

"I was hustling in as you hustled her out . . . so?"

"So what?"

"So, who is she?"

Brendon paused, put his hand under his T-shirt and scratched his stomach, looked out at the lake. Finally, he said, "Would you just lay off?"

A tense moment passed before Ross replied, "What're you mad about? She's great lookin' and I'm curious, perfectly natural."

"I don't want to talk about it, okay?"

"Fine," said Ross, standing up and moving toward the door. "I don't need your version anyway," he shot back.

"Yeah?" said Brendon, curious now himself. "Why not?"

"Because," Ross answered, pointing to his brow, speaking in his all-purpose Eastern European accent, "the Great Gambini sees all and knows all."

Brendon had to smile. "Uh-huh," he said. "I suppose."

"So you just *try* hoarding your petty secrets and delusions."

Ross was halfway out the door when Brendon called, "I'll do fine with both. What're you doing?"

"Fishing now, but this afternoon we're setting up a three-on-three tournament, enough for at least five teams."

"Good."

"You interested? You could dominate these guys," Ross said encouragingly.

"No thanks."

"Okay. Had your chance to get in at ground level."

"Yeah, well . . ." Brendon made a dismissive gesture, like So what?

Ross took another step out, then looked back once more.

"Something else?" said Brendon.

"The girl?"

"Her name is Courtney Holmes."

"Classy," said Ross, nodding. "Fine. Very very fine." He smiled and disappeared out the door.

•　•　•

Brendon had already finished breakfast when the phone rang, giving him a start. He glanced at his watch, saw it was exactly ten A.M.

After three more rings he hesitantly lifted the receiver and offered a monotone, guarded "Hello."

"Brendon?" A girl's voice.

"Yes," he replied.

"I wake you up?"

It was her, Courtney. He couldn't believe it. He was tongue-tied.

"I hope not," she continued.

When he again failed to respond, she asked, "Are you there?"

"Uh-huh. Just real surprised."

"Well, I said I'd call, try to talk you into working."

"You asked your dad?"

"That's why I called right away. This is unreal, but he knows you."

"What? How?"

"Philip knows who you are because he was friends with your parents."

"When?"

"In college, I guess. He worked summers at some resort here, the same one your mom did. Your dad used to camp there, organize the parties. They were all friends."

"Unbelievable," Brendon said.

"A real coincidence," said Courtney. "Is your mom around? Philip wants to say hello."

"She's at school, Sievers."

"Weaving? Quilting?"

"Weaving, I think. You know about that place?"

"I want to take a class there some day."

Brendon knew what he wanted to ask next, but he was reluctant to bring up the subject. Finally, he chose to go straight at it: "Does your dad know what happened to mine?"

"Yes. He even knew you were coming here, but not exactly when."

"How'd he know *that?*"

"In a small town people share."

"They talk."

"Makes you feel more secure, though. Like you belong, and somebody cares."

"That's optimistic."

"It's summer. You're supposed to be optimistic."

Brendon grimaced but said nothing.

"So, will you help?"

Brendon looked at his watch. "When?"

"Right away. Like now," she answered. "We're ready."

"You sure it's okay? With your dad, I mean."

"We're both *using* you, if that's what you're thinking."

Brendon froze, pulled way back.

"I mean," she continued, "you don't come over, poor old Philip gets the brunt of it. And I'm fair game for that creepy Clayton. He knows where I live. So gimme a break, okay?"

When Brendon said nothing, Courtney tried, "You got plans or what?"

"Uh-uh."

"Then here's your chance, a meaningful activity."

". . . Okay," he said at last.

"Good," she answered.

"You starting right now?"

"Five minutes ago."

"I'll be there."

But Brendon felt vaguely threatened. He had wanted to avoid obligations, and already he'd compromised.

• • •

At first Brendon planned to take the canoe over. But he decided against it when he realized how stupid he'd look and self-conscious he'd feel paddling all the way up to Courtney's while she watched with her father. So he rode his bike instead.

With the fresh, cool morning air on his face, Brendon found the trip to the log cabin pleasant and easy—until he turned onto the gravel surface of Bay Point Road. That quarter-mile was treacherous. When he had finally coasted down

Courtney's driveway and parked his bike, Brendon stood still and listened. He could hear their voices drifting up from the beach.

Brendon came around the cabin and found himself face-to-face with Courtney and her father. They were looking over the skiff, which now rested upside down on sawhorses.

"Oh hi!" called out Courtney, coming at Brendon. Her dad followed.

Brendon waved, advanced.

"You're Brendon," said Courtney's father, extending a large, strong hand. "Philip Holmes," he announced. Brendon gripped his hand, gave it a couple manly pumps.

"Did it float?" Brendon asked, nodding toward the skiff, ending the handshake.

"Took water and nose-dived almost immediately," answered Philip.

"Oh."

"We're trying to decide if we can save her in time for the race."

Brendon scanned the twelve-foot, square-bow, flush-deck wooden boat, its red hull and white topsides still holding paint, just barely in places. He walked around it, noticed the mast and lateen-rigged sail off to one side. He glanced again at the skiff. On the stern, stenciled carefully in white script, was the boat's name, *Dues*.

"Dues," said Brendon. "Like in union dues?"

"Sort of," Philip replied. "And you know how those work."

Brendon shrugged, looked to Courtney for help, uncertain of Philip's meaning.

"You don't have a choice about paying them," Philip explained. "But it's better for you if you want to pay."

"Courtney said you built it."

"A long time ago," Philip replied. "When I was a kid, very young."

"How long ago?"

"Maybe too long."

"He wants to know how old it is," said Courtney.

"Twenty-five years," Philip answered. "At least. I think I was sixteen. One day I told my dad I wanted to learn to sail. He said, 'Great. Get a plan, build a boat, learn. Pay your dues.' So I did. I still have the blueprints somewhere. The whole thing was done with just three four-by-eight sheets of quarter-inch plywood. And nearly all the other parts came from the garage, the lumberyard, the hardware store."

Brendon looked more closely at *Dues*, noticed the four-inch brass door hinge that held the rudder in place, the clothesline hook on the bow serving as the mooring line chock, the half-aluminum, half-wood spars.

"Of course, he was testing me," Philip continued. "He figured that if I followed through and finished he'd help me when it was time to move up."

"Did he?"

"With a vengeance. He got so interested in it himself that pretty soon we had a twenty-six-foot sloop only he could sail and afford to maintain. He spent most of his time there after he retired."

"Does he still sail it?"

"He died a couple years ago."

"Oh." Brendon glanced off, felt a little embarrassed. He'd forgotten that Courtney had already told him about her grandparents. He searched for a suitable comment but couldn't come up with one. Instead he tried, "How big is the sail?" He pointed to the rolled white sheet.

"Seventy-five."

"Same as a Sunfish."

"Exactly. You know about all boats."

"A little. My dad . . ."

Philip waited a moment more, then said, "I'm really sorry about your father, Brendon. We were close friends once. He was an interesting, very complicated guy. Popular and fun."

Brendon nodded, stared at the ground.

"So your dad took you sailing?" Philip asked.

"He wanted to," said Brendon. "We always planned to get one, but . . ."

"So you haven't tried it."

Brendon knew Philip was doing his best to keep the conversation going, keep it focused, and he liked him for that.

"I went with some guys from school," Brendon said. "One's got a little Hobie Cat, the other a Sunfish."

"Then you're a veteran, and certainly *qualified*."

Brendon looked up, met Philip's gaze, his smile. Brendon asked, "Qualified for what?"

"To join the *Dues* 'Power Repair and Racing Team,' if you want."

"Nice pitch, Philip," said Courtney.

"We need help," replied Courtney's father. "A full crew plus backup."

"I really don't know enough," Brendon said, gesturing at the skiff, the peeling paint.

"Call it an educational opportunity, then," Philip suggested. "Hands-on vocational training."

Brendon smiled.

"He's kidding," said Courtney. "I hope you see that." Before Brendon could respond, she added, "You don't want to get stuck, fine."

"I wasn't kidding," teased Philip. "Look at me. I'm *old*.

Out of shape and desperate. I want to race in a week. I need *youth*, the Pepsi generation."

"What'll it take?" asked Brendon.

"To get her restored?" Philip said.

"Uh-huh."

"Here's the diagnosis." Philip began by pointing to the deck joints. "Along the lower freeboard we've got leaky seams. I'll have to pick up some good marine putty for those. The rudder and centerboard need to be sanded, stained, and sealed. And the hull has to be checked for dry rot, then scraped, sanded, primed, and painted."

"How do you check for dry rot?" asked Brendon.

"Probe," answered Philip. "With a screwdriver." He picked one up and said, "Like this." He began poking at the hull where the paint had blistered, baring the wood. "Look for soft spots. You can handle it."

"Just like that," said Courtney. "No sweat."

"Lotta sweat," said Philip.

"You really think it's worth the time?" asked Courtney. "And money?"

Philip gave her a withering look that Brendon thought was genuine, no fooling. "Absolutely," Philip responded.

"What about the sail?" asked Brendon.

"That's in good shape," said Philip, turning his gaze to the lateen rig lying on the beach.

That's when Brendon decided to ask, "How come the spars are half aluminum, half wood?"

"Simple. I couldn't find the tubing in fourteen-foot lengths. That," said Philip, pointing to the rigging, "is called making do. I even made the sail, turned me into quite a seamstress."

"Really?"

"Oh yes."

"I didn't know that," said Courtney, surprised.

"But it was truly embarrassing to go into that fabric store in Sturgeon Bay and order the ten yards of 'nurse's uniform Dacron' called for in the directions."

Both Courtney and Brendon smiled.

"The material's still okay?" Brendon asked.

"It hasn't been in the sun and hasn't stretched."

All three of them stood staring at the hull now.

"So what's first?" asked Courtney.

"The grunt work," said Philip.

"Scraping?" said Courtney.

"And sanding. Probing."

"Which are you going to do?" Courtney asked her father.

"Me? I'm going shopping, pick up the stuff you'll need."

"You're all class, Philip," said Courtney, again with a tone that confused Brendon. There was a hard, sarcastic edge to it.

"I'll be right back," Philip assured them.

"Of course I *trust* you," Courtney responded, really putting him on the spot now.

"That's good," Philip answered calmly. "That's all I've ever wanted." He gave Brendon a little nod and began walking up to the cabin. Soon he disappeared around back and they heard him starting the Jeep, watched him pull out and drive off.

"You don't mess around," Brendon said without thinking.

"No. I can't afford to," Courtney replied. "Not with him."

"I'm sorry," Brendon said. "It's none of my business."

Courtney shrugged, looked away. Then she turned to face Brendon again, smiled gamely, and asked, "Which do you want?"

"Which what?"

"Sanding or scraping or probing."

"You pick first."

Courtney reached for the electric sander. "This is easier, right?"

"Hand me that screwdriver," said Brendon.

And the restoration of *Dues* began.

10

Brendon worked on one side of the boat, Courtney on the other.

"Have you sailed much?" asked Brendon as he slid the sharp-edged scraper gently along the hull, pulling off bubbled paint. He then checked for dry rot the way Philip had showed him. He was glad not to find any. He allowed himself a little optimism the further down the hull he went. He began hoping the project would succeed.

"I took a few lessons at summer camp when I was twelve," replied Courtney.

"But you never sailed this?" he said, tapping the skiff with his scraper.

"I never even saw this, till last week." Courtney clicked on the deafening belt-sander and worked over a few bad spots. "Know what?" she said, leaning close to inspect her work.

"What?"

"Maybe I shouldn't do this till after we fix the nails. I almost shredded the belt."

So together Brendon and Courtney went over the entire boat, pounding in and setting loose nails, sometimes replacing them. When that was done, they put in a noisy hour of scraping and sanding. Conversation was suspended.

Finally, Courtney shut off the sander and announced, "Break time."

"So soon?"

"We keep it up, Philip won't get to help. Man deserves his chance, right?"

Brendon stood back, looked down the hull. "We are making progress," he said.

"I just want to see him sweat," said Courtney.

"Your dad?"

"Philip, yes."

"He looks strong, like he could work hard."

"He used to be a fat slob, you want the truth."

"Yeah?"

"When he left."

"Uh-huh."

"From drinking so much. I bet he went two-sixty."

"Then he's lost a lot," answered Brendon, thinking Philip Holmes looked middle-aged blocky at most.

"He's still losing, wants to be down to one-eighty by the end of summer. Like you."

"That'll take discipline. He's still pretty big."

"That part of him makes me happy, the self-discipline. It's got something to do with his success at writing, getting control of that. He seems really different, but I can't let myself trust the differences, not yet."

Brendon looked out across the bay, over Porte des Morts toward mainland. "Why are you telling me all this personal stuff?" he dared to ask. "I mean we hardly know . . ." Brendon let the comment drift.

Courtney didn't respond right away. "I just feel I can

64

be open with you," she said at last, "like we have a lot in common."

"Yeah? Like what?"

"I'll tell you, eventually. But I don't talk this way with just anybody, that's what you're worried about. I can't afford to."

"Look, I didn't mean—"

"Maybe," interrupted Courtney, "it's because our parents were friends, you know?"

Brendon looked over at her, shrugged.

"Should I shut up?" asked Courtney.

He saw she was trying to smile.

"It seems too easy," he said. "The way you can talk about everything."

"Well, it's not easy, unless someone's listening, someone you think you respect."

"Then I'll listen," said Brendon.

"Thanks," she said. "I'll listen too."

He nodded.

"So ask me anything," she said. "I'll tell you."

Brendon thought it over, decided to start simply. He asked, "That Jeep, is it yours?"

"Uh-uh. Philip's."

"How'd you get up here?"

"Some friends. There's a bunch that have places on the mainland. Lots of Chicago people come up here. They brought me all the way to Northport and Philip met me there, took me across on the ferry."

"That was nice."

"Yeah, it was. A good way to start. Gave him a chance to show off all he's learned about the island."

Before Brendon could ask another question, the Jeep returned. Philip raced it down the gravel drive, sliding to a stop. He emerged from behind the cabin with two shopping bags full of materials.

"Brought some pop!" he called out.

"Good timing!" Courtney yelled back.

Philip carried the bags down to the work site. "Nice job," he remarked, looking closely at *Dues*. "Super."

"Are we done?" asked Courtney.

"Are you?" Philip said, glancing at Brendon, who stared at Courtney. "Seems like it to me," concluded Philip. "That wasn't so bad."

"Easy for you to say," teased Courtney. "What next?"

"I'll putty the cracks and nail-holes," said Philip. "After that we'll let 'er set, see if the putty takes and doesn't shrink."

"When do we paint?" Courtney wondered.

"Maybe tomorrow. It depends."

"Same color scheme?"

"That okay? I got sentimental in the hardware store." Philip pulled the cans of top-grade marine enamel from one of the bags. Red and white labels.

"New name?" asked Courtney.

"No way," Philip said bluntly.

"Well, it is your boat . . . *Dad*."

Brendon glanced at Courtney, not liking her tone again.

"But I'll share it," replied Philip, smiling now, salvaging the conversation as far as Brendon was concerned.

"Will you trust us to paint it?" Courtney asked.

"Another tough one," said Philip. "You can prime it," he offered. "We'll see how that goes."

"Our big break," Courtney said to Brendon, who felt suddenly tense. Maybe because Courtney was using him now to team up on her father. Or were they all on the same team? Brendon couldn't tell.

"Brendon," said Philip, "did your dad ever tell you about crossing the Door?"

"Some story."

"Everybody's got a Mike Turner story. He really enjoyed himself up here."

For an instant Brendon thought Philip had the wrong Michael Turner. Playing around, *enjoying himself*, was not something Brendon had seen his father do very often. Work himself, yes. Overwork himself at the family's expense, all the time.

"I'm talking about the canoes," said Philip.

"What?" said Brendon, paying attention now.

"The canoes your dad borrowed? I was the guy who left them unlocked that night, available. Up at Westwind Resort." Philip pointed north, up the coast.

"You get in trouble, too?"

"Nearly lost my job. I would have if the canoes had been wrecked or sunk. But your dad saved them, and me. He was a good man," said Philip.

Brendon said nothing, just stared at *Dues*.

"Know what this really is?" Philip asked, placing a hand on the skiff.

Brendon shook his head.

"Therapy."

"Everything's therapy," added Courtney. "To you."

Philip shot her a dark glance, but softened it almost immediately. "There's a way for everyone," he said. "Lots of ways."

There was an awkward silence that Philip broke with,

"Let's go over it one more time before I putty, okay?"

Brendon and Courtney nodded.

• • •

In many ways it had been a golden morning and early afternoon for Brendon. As he pedaled back to his cottage he felt buoyant and eager for the first time in months. He was amazed how easy it was to talk and work with Courtney, a girl he'd just met. He wondered if anybody could have done as well as he had. Could Ross? Brendon didn't think so, and that made him happy. Strange thoughts.

Before he left Courtney's, her father had invited him back tomorrow for the priming and painting. "Unless I wake up at midnight and feel compelled to go out and do it all myself," Philip added.

The only thing bothering Brendon was the tension that sometimes flashed between father and daughter. Brendon could understand her being bitter, but he also knew she recognized the changes in Philip. She wanted to believe in him. But she probably wished he had made his improvements at home, *been there* for her.

As for himself, Brendon was coping.

• • •

On Saturday, Courtney called at eleven A.M.

"It's prime time," she said.

"You mean *priming* time."

"Whatever. It's still work."

"Maybe not all work."

"A little fellowship? That'd be nice."

"You want me to help?"

"Pure telepathy. Put a rush on it, okay?"

• • •

68

Brendon decided to take the canoe this time. He was thinking they could maybe drift around the bay while the prime coat dried, give them something to do. Brendon left the cottage feeling far less apprehensive than yesterday.

When he rounded the point and entered Figenschau Bay, he could see *Dues*, but not Courtney or her father. Brendon made for shore, paddling briskly.

Just before he landed the canoe, he spotted Courtney. And the sight of her dazzled him. She came out of the cabin in a white one-piece swimming suit. Over it she wore white cotton running shorts. On her feet were jogging shoes, also white. Her tan seemed to glow against her outfit. She saw him and waved.

"*Very* nice timing!" she called out.

Brendon smiled up at her as he dragged the canoe onto the beach.

"Is it ready?" he asked, pointing at *Dues*.

"Uh-huh. The seams are tight. According to Admiral Philip anyway."

"He around?"

"Off doing errands. He said priming is so easy we couldn't possibly screw it up."

"Show of confidence," said Brendon.

"And trust."

So they went at it and it was an easy job, the old skiff soaking up the primer so quickly that by the time they finished the first coat *Dues* was ready for a second. The warm, dry air and soft breeze were perfect conditions for painting. With the second coat completed and with Philip still away, Brendon asked Courtney, "You need more exercise?"

She followed his gaze to the canoe.

"Okay," she said. "Where to?"

"Just out and around. A pleasure cruise."

"Let's go."

As they paddled leisurely across the bay—Courtney in the bow, Brendon astern—he watched the tense and flex of her muscles, arms and shoulders, the flutter of her hair, the honeyed perfection of her skin, and he dared to say it: "You look great."

She turned then and gave him a soft smile. She said, "Thank you. You look okay yourself."

And there it was . . . the start of something.

"I should've brought the fishing rods," said Brendon quickly, wanting to shift her attention now.

She kept smiling. "Maybe some other time," she said. "I'd enjoy that."

"Okay," said Brendon, paddling again.

"I think maybe we're on the same frequency, you know?"

"Uh-huh."

"I heard that once."

"What?"

"How sometimes people can tell things to strangers they won't tell their families or friends, or even themselves."

Brendon nodded, stared at her, thought: That's the truth.

Suddenly Brendon's peace was shattered.

"Hey!" hollered Philip Holmes from shore. "Nice piece of work!" He was pointing at *Dues*. Then he waved them in.

As they neared the cabin, Philip began conversing, long before they landed the canoe.

"It looks terrific! Everything took, tight as a drum."

Brendon and Courtney smiled back.

"I want to get a coat of paint on before we go, Courtney."

"Go where?" she asked, as the bow touched shore and she climbed out to pull it up far enough for Brendon to step off. Philip came down to help her.

"The interview," he said. "You didn't see my note?"

"Uh-uh."

Philip glanced at his watch. "You still have plenty of time to get ready while I paint."

"Ready for *what*?" Courtney asked sharply.

Philip waited a moment to answer, seeming to collect himself, his patience. "Some guy from the *Milwaukee Journal*," he began, "wants to do a story about us, life on the island. He needs some shots. That okay? A little fame and fortune."

"Who gets the fortune?" she asked.

"Fifty-fifty."

"I imagine," she teased.

"You don't want to go, I'll make excuses."

"What kind of shots?"

"Sitting around all the famous landmarks, looking native."

"Okay." Then turning to Brendon she asked, "That all right with you?"

He was so surprised at being consulted that he stammered a quick, "N-no problem."

When no one else spoke, Brendon said, "Well, I better be going. Have fun."

Philip gave him a friendly nod.

"Unless you want me to help with the painting," Brendon added.

"I've got to do *some* of this myself," said Philip. "We've exploited you enough."

Brendon tried to find a positive way to take Philip's comment, but couldn't. He waved to Courtney, then headed for the canoe.

"Be home tomorrow," said Philip.

"Why?" asked Brendon.

"Just don't wander off."

Brendon waited for further explanation, but none followed. So he waved again and pushed the canoe into the shallows.

11

On Sunday Brendon woke to a ringing phone. He bolted up, his breathing fast and shallow. The ringing stopped. His mother or Ross had been there to make it stop. Where had he been? Asleep. At least he hadn't been dreaming, not *that* dream anyway, but still he unraveled.

Brendon took a deep breath and eased himself back down. He reached for his watch, was surprised at how late it was, already past ten. He laced his hands behind his head, closed his eyes, and breathed evenly, slowly, trying to relax.

The first Brendon heard of the picnic was when Anne looked in and told him, "Don't make any plans for this afternoon and evening."

"Why not?" Brendon asked.

"Philip Holmes just called," Anne replied, as if that cleared up everything.

"What'd he *say*?"

"You don't know? He didn't mention it to you yesterday?"

"No."

"We're having a picnic, a reunion at School House Beach. Today."

"Who's 'we'?"

"Some of the people Dad and I knew when we were young and worked here. The whole thing is Philip's idea. He's very encouraged by how well you and he and Courtney are getting along, so he thought maybe the generations should mix."

"Great," said Brendon without enthusiasm.

"Have you been back there yet, School House Beach?"

"No. Ross has."

"Remember it?"

"Barely."

. . .

Brendon had wanted to get up then and call Courtney, ask what she thought of the picnic idea. But he realized it wasn't worth pursuing. The thing would happen no matter what he felt. So he decided to try it, take as much as he could, then wander off as early as possible, especially if things began to draaaggggg.

. . .

A few hours later, when the Turners arrived at School House Beach, most of the others were already there. Brendon became alarmed when they had to drive right through the island cemetery to get to the park. He hadn't remembered that detail. Ross was the yakker on this trip, telling about all the fun he'd had swimming here last week with the basketball players.

"They usually can't get in the water until late July or early August," Ross was saying, "but because of the warm spring they've already put out the diving raft."

Brendon strained to look past Ross and out the front windshield, caught a glimpse of the beach and pontoon raft. The beach was all stones—small, smooth, round white ones.

"See those stones, Brendon," remarked Anne.

"Sure," he replied.

"Remember now?"

He shrugged, said nothing.

"The last time we were here Dad called those the *ultimate babysitter*. Remember how long you two stood there trying to get the perfect skip while Dad hollered instructions about form and balance?"

"How long?" said Brendon.

"Hours, I can recall that much," Anne said. "We had the nicest time, just watching the water and resting and talking, and being amazed by your persistence, both of you. You just wouldn't give up. You don't remember that?"

"Sort of," said Brendon, hoping for a quick end to this maudlin gaze down Memory Lane.

Anne drove the car across the small lot, nosing it under a canopy of boughs formed by some huge white pines. No sooner had she killed the engine than Ross was out and hurrying toward the beach.

"Ross!" Anne called after him. But it was no use. He was gone. "Thanks for your help, Ross," she said to herself, glancing back at Brendon.

"I'll carry them," offered Brendon, referring to the beach blankets, the jam-packed cooler, the cumbersome picnic basket.

Brendon had just come around the car with his hands full when Courtney appeared before him and said, "Let me take something."

"The blankets," said Brendon. And she lifted them off the cooler, which Brendon had to carry with both hands. "Thanks," he said, and began walking. "Where to?"

"Aren't you going to introduce me?" asked Courtney.

Brendon stopped dead, embarrassed. "Sorry," he said. "Mom?"

"Yes," said Anne, coming closer, smiling.

"This is Courtney Holmes. Anne Turner," Brendon said, looking at Courtney.

The two women exchanged hi's and smiles, and then all three began working their way down to the picnic area. Philip Holmes had already staked out their space, and he greeted Brendon with a handshake, Anne with a hug.

"I've been in the water," said Courtney to Brendon, "and it's great. Once you get used to it."

"Cold?"

"But not like it's supposed to be."

"That's what my brother was saying."

"Is he here?" asked Courtney, looking around.

"Over there," Brendon gestured with a nod, sending Courtney's attention to the swimming area where Ross had shed his sweats, was down to his trunks, and had both feet in the water. He quickly moved out far enough to make a plunging dive that turned into a frantic crawl as he tried to get used to the water and make it out to the diving raft.

"Let me get rid of this," said Brendon. He set down the cooler and headed for the beach himself with Courtney.

"Be careful," Anne called after him.

He waved back.

"What's his name, your brother?" asked Courtney.

". . . Gambini," said Brendon.

"No. You're kidding."

"Ask him."

When they emerged from the woods and were able to take in the whole beach, Brendon was pleased by what he saw. The large horseshoe bay was lined almost entirely with the white stones. The water was a gorgeous blue-green, clear and placid.

76

"Isn't this beautiful?" said Courtney.

"Uh-huh. So far, anyway," Brendon replied. "You know any of these people?" Brendon was looking at the dozen or so adults that made up their party. He didn't see many kids, only two very young ones.

"I've met a few. They all seem really nice. And they're all so anxious to meet you and talk to your mother. Your dad must've been a real character, the stories about him, Mr. Daredevil."

Brendon stared at Courtney, chewed his gum more slowly, struggled for a polite response.

Courtney read him perfectly. "You don't want me to talk about him, just say so," she remarked.

"I don't always know this guy they're talking about," said Brendon.

Courtney looked down, then brought her eyes to Brendon's, gave him a small shrug. "That can happen," she said.

"Want to swim?" he asked, looking around nervously.

"Okay."

But before Brendon could get out of his jeans and down to the trunks he was wearing underneath, Anne called to him. Brendon walked back toward the picnic area with Courtney, meeting Anne halfway. "Could you let me introduce you to some old friends?" she asked as they approached the group.

"Damn old!" said one sort of paunchy, balding guy with a calming, crooked smile.

Brendon gave Courtney a look, then turned and faced the crowd.

Anne presented her son to a good half-dozen couples, all of whom had known his father, all of whom looked at him with cheerful curiosity, all of whom had nothing but good things to say about both his parents.

"And he's authentic," said Philip Holmes, nodding at Brendon. "I've already seen how smart he is and how good he works. He's Mike and Annie's, all right."

Everyone had quite a laugh about that, but Brendon didn't know what to make of "Annie." A little too cozy, he thought. Just as Brendon was going to excuse himself and return to the beach, Courtney asked Philip where he put the cooler; she wanted a Coke. "Over there," her dad said, and pointed to a cluster of ice chests lined up on a picnic table.

Before she'd taken a step, the paunchy, balding guy, Mr. Meredith or Merrimeck, something like that, said, "Have one yourself, Phil!" The guy was holding up a can of beer. Brendon happened to be looking at Courtney, who stood frozen in place, staring, watching her father.

"No thanks, Nicko," said Philip Holmes quietly.

"*Huh?*" roared Nicko, who was already a little sloshed himself. "What'd he say?" Nicko did his surprised act, his eyes wide open, his right palm spread on his chest. "I don't believe my *ears!*" he continued. "Did Phil Holmes really, actually, just turn down a free beer? C'mon, pinch me," Nicko said to his wife.

A few people laughed, but very self-consciously.

"What next?" joked Nicko, on a roll, winking at Philip.

"Health," said Philip. "Maybe happiness."

There was an awkward pause as the drift of Philip's reply began making sense to Nicko. "Oh my god," he said at last, understanding the situation. "Hell, Phil, I didn't know." The man was genuinely embarrassed. He backpedaled a couple steps. "On the wagon, huh?"

Philip shrugged graciously, nodded. "You could say that."

"Well geez, I'm sorry. Lemme go behind the biffy and try

to get my foot outa my goddam mouth, okay?"

"That's all right, Nick," said Philip. "Forget it."

All the while this exchange took place, Brendon had kept an eye on Courtney. When the scene ended, and the two of them started to cut back through the woods, heading for the beach again, Brendon said, "I couldn't help noticing . . ."

"Noticing what?"

"How you looked at your dad just now. You didn't blink."

"I was amazed."

"Why?"

She stopped walking, turned, and faced Brendon, said, "I never actually saw him or heard him turn down a drink before. *Never.* I don't know if I can trust it, what I just saw."

"Why?"

"It takes me back to counseling."

She looked Brendon in the eye. He gave her an encouraging nod.

"I'll never forget it," she continued, "one particular session. Things were going their usual nowhere—"

"*You* went to counseling," he blurted, cutting in before he could stop himself. "Sorry," he said.

"That's okay," she said. "We tried all kinds of it, but nothing was . . . *blunt* enough. Until we met this one guy. The session I'm thinking of started like all the others, with Philip giving his standard circle of excuses and rationalizations. Poor Philip Holmes, all kinds of problems. He explained how other counselors told him he suffered 'acute job dissatisfaction' and thus he had a 'negative self-image' because he'd been 'victimized by mid-life crisis' and 'failure ideation' and an 'insufficient support network.' He wasn't 'in touch with his feelings' and was working off 'bad vibes.' You should've *heard* him," Courtney said. "The man could put on a real sideshow, and I've been through it so often even I can do the routine."

"Then what?"

"Right in the middle of it, the counselor says, 'Man, you've been to *all* of them, haven't you!' Philip looks off a little and says, 'All what?' And the guy says, 'All the phony-baloney California Kung-Fu therapy groups ever organized.' "

Brendon smiled, he couldn't help it.

"It's funny now, maybe," she said. "But not then."

"Sorry."

"Don't be. This is the best part. Philip's looking all hurt and pathetic when the counselor says, 'The problem here is alcohol. It's that obvious and that simple.' You know what Philip said next?"

Brendon shook his head.

"He said, 'Alcohol's the solution.' Then the counselor really opened up on him, both barrels. He said, 'Mr. Holmes, I've already had it with you and your gutless lies.'

"I thought Philip was going to get up and hit him or something. But instead he put on this little look of superiority, like he'd just gotten to the guy somehow, won a point, you know?

"Then just as Philip was about to make some snide comment, the counselor jumps in and says, 'Booze *kills*, Mr. Holmes, and I know because I've been there. Eventually it'll kill you. And I can see it's already killed plenty. Has it killed any important relationships, Mr. Holmes? Has it killed any business opportunities?'

"Philip tried to get defensive, but the guy cut him off with, 'You do like to *kill*, don't you, Mr. Holmes? And you do kill *anything*, don't you? DON'T YOU!' I mean by now the counselor is really yelling, and I was almost ready to side with

Philip, just to get this guy off his back. But when I looked at him, Philip . . ."

"Yeah?"

"The counselor had his attention, his complete, undivided attention. That's when he called Philip 'a self-centered jerk who's lost the courage to look for solutions.' "

Stunned by that line, Brendon managed to ask, "What'd your dad say then?"

Courtney didn't answer, lost inside herself suddenly, like she didn't hear him.

"What happened after that?" Brendon pressed, really interested now.

"Philip ran away." She found Brendon's eyes, held them with her pained stare. "The next week he moved out," she said.

"To get help?"

"No. That didn't come until later. He left us because he . . ."

"What?" Brendon asked softly, trying to make it easier, to help her say it, get it out in the open if that's what she wanted.

"He told us later that he left because he knew he'd killed *us*. As a family we were dead because of him."

"Was it true?"

"I don't know. I still don't. But *he* was convinced. So he gave up on us."

"What's your mom think?"

"She was relieved, glad to have him out. It must've been much worse than I realized."

"But he didn't go right into treatment or something?"

"Not for a long time, months, after he was sure he'd lose his job, but just in time to save his writing. He was hearing from some publishers, so he tried to get clean, make it possible to concentrate on a book and finish. When he finally got help he went to that same counselor, the guy who told him off. The counselor made him join a group, told him he had to share and be honest, but he wouldn't have to fight himself alone anymore."

Brendon listened carefully, startled by the feeling that every word was for him, applied to his life somehow. The feeling scared him. He asked, "You know what I still don't get?"

Courtney shook her head.

"I can't tell if you really like him. I mean, you seem to, but then you bring up all this stuff."

"I'm trying to like him. He's my father. But he's an addict. And like the counselor said, 'You can't be an addict and be anything else.' "

Brendon stared back at her, moved. Something's better than nothing, he nearly said, even an addict. But he wisely backed off. Instead, he suggested, "Let's swim awhile, okay? Try to unwind."

"Good idea," she said, "because it'll get worse if you keep me talking."

Yet that's precisely what he wanted. Brendon had the feeling she knew things he needed to know.

"C'mon. We do need to swim," she said.

Barefoot, they walked gingerly down the stony shore, nearly stumbling a few times when a pebble pushed just right against some tender spot. In the water, the stones were not only small and round but slippery. When Courtney and Brendon got the depth they needed to swim, they went for the pontoon raft, where they met Ross.

Just as Courtney neared the platform, Ross reached for

her and said, "Here, let me help."

Courtney gripped Ross's hand, pulling herself up onto the raft. Brendon lifted himself effortlessly, his muscles taut from the vigorous swim out.

"This is him?" Courtney asked Brendon, nodding at Ross. The three of them were alone on the raft.

Brendon said, "Uh-huh. So go on, ask him."

"Ask me what?" said Ross.

"Is your name really Gambini?" Courtney inquired, giving him her best heart-melting smile.

"Well, no, I . . ."

"I've already told her," said Brendon. "Secret's out, okay?" He was enjoying this rare chance to goof on his clever little brother.

"No," Ross tried again, "I—"

"Watch yourself," Brendon said to Courtney. "He sees all and knows all."

"Must be fun," she said. "All that power."

"Well, yeah," Ross concurred.

Courtney said, "I thought so."

"Is the board any good?" asked Brendon.

"Try it," Ross suggested.

So Brendon did. The board had no spring, and the lake bottom was a good twenty feet below. After the first few feet of surface water, the temperature dropped drastically. Still, they had fun taking turns, trying lots of ambitious but badly executed dives. No one really noticed the silver-flecked runabout pulling skiers back and forth across the harbor.

Then suddenly the boat came racing right at the diving raft. It was only a few feet away, and not pulling a skier, when it swerved dangerously close, veered off, and sent a wave of spray over everyone on the raft, including Ross, who'd just returned after his last dive. Brendon got the brunt of the dousing.

As the boat turned and came slowly back toward the pontoon raft, Brendon could see the driver clearly, Clayton Wills. Brendon was ready to jump for the boat and kick hell out of Wills when Ross piped up with, "Nice shot, Claymore. You're a real talent."

"Easy, chump," said Wills, standing now as the runabout idled, the powerful engine gurgling. He had two guys with him that Brendon didn't recognize.

Then Wills said to Ross, "You know this guy?" He jerked his head at Brendon.

"Sort of."

"Can he talk?"

"Depends."

"On?"

"His audience, if he's got one."

Wills turned to Brendon, said, "I'm all ears, Slick."

Brendon wanted to tell him to go snap his bean in private, take the edge off. Or maybe put his brain back on ice, something he'd understand, let him know he was way past the limit. But Courtney was there, and by now Brendon was mute with rage.

Wills shook his head. "Nothing today, huh Slick?" Then to Courtney, "How about you, Sweet? You speaka mah language?"

Behind Wills, one of his buddies sniggered.

"C'mon, Babe. Join us. Wanna ski? You don't know how, I'll teach you."

Brendon had gauged the distance and would've made his move, jumped all over Wills, had Courtney not checked him

84

with, "Like you've got the playmates you need already, okay?"

This time it was Ross who guffawed.

Wills tried to give him The Look. "Next game, chump," he warned.

"Riiiiight, Claymore," Ross answered. "Why don't you go fondle your throttle and buzz off."

"Later, chump!" yelled Wills, his face red now. "Count on it." Then he looked at Brendon, said, "Bye-bye Slick," and gunned the engine, sending a rooster-tail spray at the raft, soaking Brendon again, who was now so upset, even breathing was difficult. Why didn't he *do* something? he asked himself. Why'd he just stand there and let the others do his fighting?

"You okay?" asked Courtney, close to him.

"Guy really wants it," said Brendon.

"C'mon, you haven't seen guys like him before?"

"Not many, not still on the loose."

"He's like a sixth-grade bully or something, only with more toys."

Brendon wanted to smile, let her know how much he appreciated her loyalty, but he couldn't manage it. This guy Wills had reached him, simple as that.

"Let's go," said Ross. "They just called us in for supper."

• • •

The painful, barefoot hike back up the beach did nothing to lighten Brendon's mood.

"Any broken glass?" called out Philip, who'd been watching their struggle.

"The stones hurt," Courtney answered. "Our soles aren't tough yet."

That made Philip Holmes laugh. "Soles aren't tough yet," he repeated. "You've got a week," he said.

Finally they returned to the picnic area, dry and ready to devour the juicy burgers and brats that Anne and Philip and the others had prepared perfectly. They all stuffed themselves, talking and laughing, watching the sun as it began sliding down behind the western rim of the bay, turning the blue sky pink, then blood red, then deep purple.

Soon bonfires were started and everyone lined up to get the makings of "s'mores"—marshmallows, graham crackers, and Hershey bars. Somewhere, over in the middle of another group, somebody played a guitar. But there were no silly campfire sing-alongs. Thank goodness, thought Brendon. No one should have to share that much schmaltz in one day.

That night, as the picnic-party broke up, Brendon was as sad as anyone to see it end. Aside from his latest confrontation with Clayton Wills, this was one of Brendon's *best times*.

While Anne drove the Pontiac out of the parking lot, she asked, "Did you guys have fun? Brendon?"

"It was okay," he answered.

Still not ready to concede anything.

12

"**C**hampagne time now!"

It was Courtney. And Monday. Early. How early, just past nine. You had to love these cool, clear nights, Brendon thought. Great sleeping weather. And he was thankful for the rest, but glad to hear Courtney's voice on the phone, early or not.

"I don't get it," Brendon said, stifling a yawn, shaking out the cobwebs.

"We're about to launch the all-new H.M.S. *Dues*. Philip is done painting and buffing, and it looks great."

"I'd like to see it."

"No choice, Captain's request."

"Huh?"

"Philip says he'll hold off launching till you get here."

". . . Okay."

"You awake? You sound a little dozy."

"I'll be all right. I'm conscious now. That swimming really took it out of me."

"Me too."

"Yeah, you really sound beat, Ms. Bright Eyes."

Courtney laughed. "I'm a morning person. So hurry up, okay? The wind is just right."

. . .

Brendon gulped a glass of juice and rushed out. He raced his bike along the winding, tree-lined turns of West Harbor Road, cutting back and forth across the traffic lanes—blind curves—to shorten his trip. He was risking disaster by charging into oncoming traffic, but feeling vaguely thrilled by the gamble. He was lucky to find himself in the right lane at just the right time, when a slow-moving station wagon came at him out of the last turn.

. . .

At the log cabin, Courtney and Philip were already down by the L-shaped dock, both in swimming suits, Courtney wearing a teal one-piece this time. Philip held the bowline and watched *Dues* bobbing in place, its white Dacron sail fluttering. They looked up at the same time when Brendon came around the cabin and waved.

When the three were together on the dock, Philip said, "You go first," to Courtney.

"You sure?" she replied. "It's your baby."

"You're my baby," said Philip with a wink, his voice full of mock sentimentality.

"Right . . . *Daddy*," Courtney joked back. She looked down at *Dues*, then over at Brendon, said, "Okay, I'll go first."

Philip and Brendon watched as Courtney climbed down into the little cockpit. Next, Philip pushed the skiff away from the dock. The sail filled, and *Dues* slid out into the bay. The gentle wind was steady from the northwest, so Courtney ran straight across the bay, came about neatly, and brought *Dues* back in.

"How is it?" asked Philip as he reached down to catch the bow, keep it from banging against the dock.

"Seems fine to me," Courtney answered, climbing out carefully. Brendon helped pull her up.

"Your turn," Philip said to Brendon.

"No," he said. "You better go. I want to watch how you handle it."

So Philip took his turn. He stumbled a little as he lowered himself in, and when he sat down heavily there wasn't much freeboard showing. He moved with none of Courtney's lithe grace. When Brendon shoved off *Dues* and the sail bulged, Philip kept it close-hauled and the skiff heeled dramatically until he hiked-out to counter the lean. Then it nearly tipped the other way. Philip quickly adjusted his position, and soon the boat was racing along at near-maximum speed.

After his run, Philip carefully brought *Dues* back and said to Brendon, "When you go, take my course and see if you notice anything about how it's cutting."

Brendon nodded, and the two of them exchanged places while Courtney held the bow. Brendon set himself in the cockpit, gripping hard both the tiller and mainsheet, prickling with anticipation and the fear of embarrassing himself on open water. Seconds later he couldn't believe how easily *Dues* sailed or how competent he felt once he was crossing the bay. As he cut to the southwest, he tried to mimic Philip's trim and course. When he thought he'd hit both and reached top speed, he sensed what Philip must have been hinting at. *Dues* was being pushed sideways a little when it took the wind full-force.

Brendon steered back to the dock and told Philip what he thought he'd discovered.

"*Exactly*," said Philip. Then he added, "Must be the centerboard. It's too short."

"You guys have it down all the way?" asked Courtney.

"Uh-huh," said Brendon. "Still is."

"We need a bigger one," remarked Philip. "Right now. The race is this week."

Courtney asked, "But won't that change the physics of the thing?"

"The physics of the thing," repeated Philip, giving his daughter a confused look.

"You make one lever bigger, longer, stronger," she went on, "don't you need to compensate the other way? To maintain balance?"

"You mean the mast?" said Brendon.

She nodded, bit her lower lip with her front teeth, and smiled.

"Honey," said Philip, "it was an aversion to physics that left me where I am today. I frankly don't know. You think we need a taller mast?"

"Maybe," she said. "And what about where it goes?"

"The step?" said Philip.

"Uh-huh."

He shrugged for emphasis. "All we can do is try a few things. I'll start with a bigger centerboard and work my way up. Sound sensible?" He was addressing Courtney.

"I guess," she replied.

"One other thing I want to try," Philip said. "This race, the Channel Challenge?"

Both Courtney and Brendon looked up, gave him their attention.

"It involves two laps, two trips over and back. On the first leg I'd like to go with you." Philip pointed to his daughter.

90

"And for the gun lap, I'll act my age and let you guys take over, okay?"

"Fine with me," Courtney answered.

"So let's see if that'll work. You first," Philip said to Courtney, helping her to board *Dues*. When Philip hunkered onto the aft deck, the stern dropped below the waterline and the cockpit flooded.

"DAD!" Courtney shrieked, grabbing the gunwales to keep from being flipped overboard.

"Oh my!" said Philip, scrambling back onto the dock, then reaching for Courtney. "I've got a ways to go yet, don't I?" Philip looked at *Dues*, then down at his thick torso. He patted his stomach. "Too many s'mores," he said.

Brendon watched Courtney hide a smile.

"Well," Philip went on, "there goes Plan A. Looks like I'll fly solo on lap one. How's that?"

"Just get us a lead," said Courtney.

"You'll have it," Philip replied, standing straighter. Then Philip turned to Brendon and asked, "You ever been to Rock Island?"

"No."

"You want to see it, and the channel that's going to challenge us?"

"Sure," replied Brendon.

"Let's go, then," said Philip.

So they pulled on jeans and packed into the CJ and headed up to Jackson Harbor on the opposite corner of the island, the far northeast side, nearly an eight-mile trip.

They pulled into the Jackson Harbor parking lot just as the little passenger ferry, *Karfi*, was landing.

"Good," said Philip. "We can see the channel up close and wander around the island a little."

Brendon remembered from his reading that Rock Island had been owned by a successful Chicago industrialist and inventor named Chester Thordarson. Thordarson's dream for the island was to build a replica of an Icelandic village there, using traditional architecture and stone construction. He made stunning progress before his death.

Brendon stared open-mouthed from the deck of the *Karfi* as they moved closer to the immense boathouse and great hall that loomed above the Rock Island dock. The channel separating the islands was not large, and looked like it would be easy to sail, thought Brendon. Under today's conditions, anyway.

As the ten-minute ride ended and the Viking Hall towered over them, Philip commented, "There's a fireplace up there big enough for five men to stand inside. Want to see it?"

"Sure," said Courtney and Brendon, nearly in unison.

On landing, the three quickly toured the massive beach-stone structure and were duly impressed by its huge arching windows and high ceilings supported by heavy timbers. They learned that Thordarson housed everything from large social gatherings to rare books in his great hall, and that the boathouse alone cost him nearly a quarter-million dollars.

"And those were 1920s dollars," Philip pointed out. "Couldn't build the foundation for that today."

"The man had a vision," said Courtney as they left.

"And plenty of imagination to make it work," said Philip.

"I'm glad they saved all this," Courtney added. "Didn't let Truman Wills turn it into condos."

Outside, they took one more long look at the Viking Hall before Philip said, "Care to take a hike?"

"Where?" asked Courtney.

Philip pointed. "The northern end. There's an old light-house there, the first one built on Lake Michigan I think, and a super view."

"Why not?" said Courtney, looking at Brendon. "You up for it?" she asked.

"Why not?" he answered, smiling now.

During the twenty-minute mostly uphill walk, Philip pointed out and named trees and wildflowers and birds.

"You're a regular trail guide," said Courtney. "Where'd you learn all that stuff?"

"Self-taught," said Philip. "I'm working on another book set in the county, but that's not the reason I've been study-ing. To know about things in nature seems more important when you live here. Understand?"

"Uh-huh," Courtney replied.

"How're you holding up?" Philip asked.

Brendon looked over and realized Philip was addres-sing him.

"Great," he said. "It's so peaceful and relaxing."

"We may meet a few other hikers, but that'll be it. Most of the visitors camp on the southeast corner."

Brendon did feel great. He was still in good shape and he knew it, a sinewy spring to his step. His legs felt stronger and stronger as the trail steepened. Finally they arrived at the lighthouse, only to find it locked. So they cut through the last few yards of woods and located the sheer cliff, the "Niagara escarpment" highlighted on the tourist map.

Brendon walked to the cliff edge and peeked over. "Must be a hundred-foot drop," he said.

"At least," said Philip. "Maybe you should step back a little," he suggested. "People have fallen."

"Saith the *parent*," Courtney blurted.

"I'm serious," said Philip.

Brendon retreated.

For a few moments they stood silently, awed by the majestic view. North of them lay St. Martins Island. To the northwest of that they could barely make out the thin line marking Michigan's upper peninsula.

"Can I tell you another story about your dad?" Philip asked quietly.

Brendon said, "Sure."

"The first time Mike came here, right to this spot, you know what he wanted to do?"

Brendon shook his head.

"Jump, be a cliff diver. He'd seen Acapulco in some movie. He said, 'It can be done, you guys. It's possible.' "

Brendon tried to smile, but it faltered.

"The guy loved a thrill, taking a chance," added Philip, looking not at Brendon but toward the horizon.

"Did he ever do it?" asked Brendon.

"What," said Philip, surprised at Brendon's question. "Jump?"

Brendon nodded.

"No, no. We talked him out of it. And that wasn't easy. He got obsessed with the idea, wanted to take depth readings, the whole bit."

Why didn't someone talk him out of taking that lousy VW back in February? wondered Brendon.

"Have you seen enough?" Philip asked.

"I guess," Brendon said.

"Me, too," added Courtney.

During the hike back to the ferry landing, Brendon talked

very little and listened even less. He was lost in thoughts about his father. Michael had preached and practiced very strict discipline and self-denial and hard work, but he also behaved recklessly way too often.

Brendon had never thought of Michael as a hypocrite before.

13

It rained hard and turned cold on Tuesday, the Fourth of July. That ruined a full day of activities. The County League amateur baseball game was rescheduled for Saturday, along with the kids' parade, the patriotic speeches, and the fireworks display. The Channel Challenge boat race was tentatively set for the fifth, but the forecasts weren't very promising. The Turner family was housebound, reading and resting, all day. There were no calls, made or received.

When dawn broke on Wednesday, Brendon awakened to the sound of wind rushing through trees near the cottage. Without even looking he was sure the wind was far too strong for a safe boat race. So he rolled over and slept another hour, until Anne woke him with an invitation. She suggested they all have breakfast at the Sunset Resort before she went off to her weaving class.

"You'll love it," she said to Brendon and Ross after both had dressed. "Thin, rolled Icelandic pancakes, lightly basted eggs, spicy pork sausage, warm cinnamon coffee cake, nine-grain toast—"

"Enough, *foul temptress*!" cried Ross, his palms pressed against his ears. "Entice me no more with such high-cal enchantments!"

96

Anne laughed. "Goodness," she said. "Is that a *no*?"

"Not really," said Ross. "Call it token resistance."

"Brendon?"

"I'm up for it."

So they went there and stuffed themselves, and afterwards Anne drove to Sievers while Ross and Brendon walked back to the cottage. They'd barely gotten in the door when Ross said, "Bren, I have to tell you something."

Ross's eerie tone put Brendon on full alert.

"Yeah?" he said.

"This Clayton Wills, he really has it in for you, don't ask me why."

"What's that mean?"

"Guy's after you."

"How do you know?"

"Ever since he found out you're my brother, he's been yappin' at me, trying to cheapshot me in the games. You know, push, shove, elbow, trip, the whole routine."

"Why didn't you tell me?"

"Cuz he's not too good at it," Ross answered, smiling. "I'm quick enough to see most of it coming. And when he gets me a little, I even it up pretty fast."

"You want me to straighten him out?"

"Naw. I can handle him on the court. The other guys side with me, too. But he's not looking to get you on any court. What I'm saying is watch out for him. Boy's real sneaky."

"I know," said Brendon.

• • •

That afternoon Courtney called. She began with, "He finished it, so we're set."

"Finished what?"

"Philip," said Courtney. "The new centerboard."

"Yeah?"

"He just tried it out and said everything's fine."

"Isn't it still too windy? Blowing pretty hard up here."

"Not here," she said. "Our bay's more protected. He just took it out a few minutes ago. That's why I'm calling."

"Why?"

"We never tried sailing together the other day."

"That's right."

"We've got to check, make sure we don't weigh too much to race."

"Or even float."

"Uh-huh."

"So we should practice."

"Exactly. How soon can you be over?"

"I'm leaving now."

"I'll make sure everything's ready."

• • •

When Brendon arrived at Courtney's he found her alone. Philip had gone off to mail some letters.

Courtney had already rigged *Dues*. Brendon joined her on the dock.

"Here goes," she said, stepping into the cockpit. "C'mon."

Brendon climbed aboard very carefully, and though the skiff sat low in the water, it remained afloat, completely functional.

"Okay so far," said Brendon.

"Now the real test," Courtney remarked as she pushed *Dues* away from the dock. The bow swung out and the wind hit the sail so hard it nearly swamped them. Only Courtney's skill with the mainsheet kept them from wiping out immediately.

"Close call," said Brendon. "Nice work."

98

"Thanks," Courtney replied, as *Dues* took a conservative tack into a far stronger wind than they'd dealt with before.

After several passes their confidence grew to the point where Brendon insisted they attempt increasingly dangerous runs. On one of them, the skiff heeled so steeply that surf washed over the deck within two inches of the cramped cockpit.

That's when Courtney said, "Back off a little, huh?"

"In a sec," Brendon answered, the wind whipping his hair around, rippling his T-shirt.

"We're at the max right now," warned Courtney.

"Just a little more," said Brendon. "I think we can get it."

"A Ulysses complex!" teased Courtney, watching the waterline.

"Huh?"

"The epic thrill seeker."

"Oh sure," said Brendon. Then easing off quickly, Brendon asked, "You like mythology?"

"That's a strange question."

"I took the course this year," said Brendon. "First fifth-hour class I haven't slept through."

"You think more about that stuff on an island, you know?"

"Uh-huh. That's what I was thinking at that cliff the other day. I felt like we were in one of those B-movies, *The Conquering Greeks*."

"Let's do our conquering in the Channel Challenge, okay? It'll depress Philip if we don't."

"Really?"

"He's a competitor," said Courtney, looking off. "Want to go in?"

"A few more runs?"

"All right."

So they took *Dues* through the paces, worked on their turns and tacks, discovered little peculiarities about the skiff. One *big* peculiarity revealed itself when Courtney leaned on the mast to free the mainsheet after a not-so-successful come about. When she placed most of her weight forward, the bow plunged, sending a wave across the deck, soaking her and flooding the cockpit. Only Brendon's quick reach and strong grip kept her from falling overboard.

"Thanks," she said, as they bailed. "Let's not forget that, okay?"

Brendon nodded and together they brought *Dues* in. After stowing the rigging and tying the boat securely, Brendon and Courtney walked around the cabin to where Brendon had parked his bike.

"That was exciting," she said.

"Uh-huh. Action-packed, for practice."

"Philip says we might race tomorrow."

"Then it's good we worked out."

"Yes."

Brendon was suddenly brain-locked.

"You know what?" she asked. "I really enjoy this, being with you."

Brendon looked away. When he finally met her gaze, she was smiling faintly. "I mean it," she said.

"I enjoy it, too," he said quietly.

Before he could come up with another line, she stepped close to him, rose on tiptoe, and kissed him lightly on the mouth. "So there," she said. "I've been wanting to try that."

Brendon reached for her, took her gently by the shoulders, and brought her in for another kiss. At first he held back a little, trying to show her he had restraint, but soon they both were holding on, getting it all, it was so good.

100

When they finally ended it, Courtney said, "What have we here?"

"Chemistry," Brendon whispered, his voice lost in his throat.

They both laughed, shy now.

"I better go," he said.

"Worried about Philip?" she teased.

"About me," he said, only half-joking.

• • •

At noon on Thursday, Brendon heard the concussion from the first skyrocket. He walked to the door of the cottage and listened. He couldn't be sure where they'd shot it off, but it seemed far away. Maybe the baseball field. The next three staccato *boom*s told him the race must be on. Courtney's phone call, which followed the final blast by seconds, confirmed his guess.

"Philip's tying down the boat right now," she said.

"Where?"

"On the Jeep. Where else?"

"You guys could lift it?"

"Hey, I'm strong. All that gymnastics."

"I know. But it's awkward."

"Would've been easier with three, if that's what you mean."

"Yeah. Next time."

"So we're coming right over to get you, okay?"

"I'll be ready."

". . . Brendon?"

"Huh?"

"You feel lucky?"

"You can win sometimes without luck," he said, paraphrasing his father.

"But you gotta *believe*."

"Believe what?"

"That everything's right, and you can handle it, the pressure, see yourself winning."

Again Brendon paused. "You believe for both of us," he suggested.

"Maybe that won't be enough. Think about it."

"We can hope."

. . .

Ten minutes after hanging up, Brendon heard Philip honking out back. He knew his mother was busy again at Sievers, but maybe Ross would take time off from basketball to watch the Channel Challenge.

When they pulled into Jackson Harbor, Brendon was stunned by the size of the crowd and the number of entrants, young and old. The rules allowed no boats longer than fourteen feet, carrying more than eighty-five square feet of sail. Of the thirty to forty boats Brendon observed, he saw craft ranging from sleek Phantoms and Sunfish to Toppers and Butterflies and Sea Devils. Brendon even spotted an old eight-foot dinghy with a tiny sail manned by two grade school kids. Somebody we can beat, he thought.

"C'mon," said Courtney, touching Brendon's forearm. "We need your help."

Philip and Brendon easily lifted *Dues* from the Jeep while Courtney carried the rigging down to the water. Philip returned to the Jeep to coil and store the rope he'd used to secure the skiff. While he was away, Brendon helped Courtney step the mast and hoist the sail on *Dues*. They'd no sooner finished when Brendon spotted Clayton Wills, *Mr. Everywhere*. He was standing knee-deep in the bay, snapping the rudder onto his black Laser.

Clayton looked up and caught Brendon staring at him. He stopped what he was doing and sloshed over to *Dues*, his smile-sneer in place.

He reached Brendon and said, "Hey Slick, quite a rig." He gave *Dues* a condescending once-over. Turning to Courtney, he said, "The hell is this, amateur hour?"

Brendon stiffened. He clenched his fists, set his arm muscles rippling. Clayton didn't notice.

Wills continued, "You really wanna be seen in this toy?"

Courtney answered, "Like, you know, I'm like the captain, okay? Daddy said."

"Oh," Wills replied, a little off balance now. Then, recovering quickly, he said, "That's cool. And you got Slick here to boss around, huh?"

At that point Brendon had had enough. He said, "C'mon." He turned, signaling Clayton to walk off with him and settle it once and for all. "You need some things explained," Brendon added, taking another step. But Wills didn't follow.

"Aw Slick," he said. "Lighten up, huh? Timing's not your thing, is it."

Brendon held his pose.

Wills said, "Okay, tell you what, Slick. You go if you want and I'll keep an eye on Sweetness here, make sure nobody violates her vessel, you know?" Then Clayton laughed. "How's that sound?" he pressed.

Brendon was ready to step up and deck him, and would have if Courtney hadn't said, "Like, that was a *joke!*" as if she'd just gotten it. "*Violate my vessel.*"

Wills rolled his eyes, but before he could comment, Philip Holmes appeared and said, "Everything set?" He totally ignored Clayton Wills.

Courtney nodded to her father.

Philip then turned abruptly, startling Wills with a withering stare, and said, "Get lost."

Wills went slack-jawed for a second, then put on the arrogant grin and pointed at Brendon. "Later, Slick," he said. Brendon frowned as Clay walked back to his boat.

"What a schmuck," said Philip.

Courtney laughed. Brendon didn't.

As Philip went around to the other side of *Dues*, Courtney said to Brendon, "Look over there."

Brendon followed her gaze to a black-haired, bulky, thick-necked man on shore, wearing a dark blue sport shirt sweat-stained at the armpits, light blue sans-belt slacks, and white loafers.

"Who's that?" Brendon asked.

"Clayton's daddy, Truman Wills, schlock developer. He'll say anything to 'move product.' "

Brendon looked closer and saw the resemblance.

"You know what he plans for this?"

Brendon turned to Courtney, found her gesturing at Rock Island. "No," he answered.

"He wants to build a causeway, the T. W. Causeway. Connect both islands to the mainland."

"What!"

"Like in Florida," she said. "The Keys. 'A bridge to the world' is how he put it."

"Can it be done?"

"He says so. Claims he's got the engineers with the know-how. Put the ferry line right out of business."

"Unbelievable." Brendon shook his head.

"A little pretentious, sure," joked Courtney.

Then Philip announced, "I think we're squared away."

"How's this going to work?" asked Brendon, staring across the strait to Rock Island, spotting the red-and-white buoy marking the far turn.

"Everyone races the first lap," said Philip. "Then the top twelve race the second for the championship."

"And you're going first?" said Courtney, giving Philip a chance to reconsider his strategy.

"Don't worry," said Philip, placing a hand on her shoulder. "You guys will get your chance. You'll have plenty of room to work."

"Such confidence," teased Courtney.

"You watch," he said with a wink. "We've got a good wind, steady from the south-southwest, and warm. We'll do fine."

So Brendon and Courtney did watch, and they were filled with awe when Philip surged to the front of the pack. He got inside position, and came out of the Rock Island turn in third place, beating to windward on the port tack. Clayton Wills was five or six boats behind, still in the top twelve.

"He must've practiced *a lot*," said Brendon, commenting on Philip's skill.

"Over and over," Courtney replied. "He really wants to make good at this for some reason."

"Show off for you," Brendon suggested.

"He's a competitor," said Courtney.

Down the backstretch, Philip gained a little on the second-place boat, a Sunfish. The top twelve were fast approaching Jackson Harbor.

From behind Brendon someone asked, "You racing?" Brendon spun around, recognizing his brother's voice.

"Pretty soon," said Brendon. "The next leg."

Courtney asked, "What're our chances, Gambini?"

Ross pressed his fingers to his forehead, squeezed his eyes shut in concentration.

"He's visiting other worlds," Brendon explained.

Finally Ross said, "Great odds." He smiled, then frowned. "But danger lurks, interlopers abound. There!" Ross pointed to Clayton and his black Laser. "Avoid impulsive acts of Wills," Ross concluded.

"Funny," said Brendon, unamused.

"That's it anyway," Ross countered. "And you can say you heard first from—"

"I hope you're wrong," said Courtney.

"Maybe," Ross conceded.

By now Philip Holmes had crossed the finish line, completing his lap in third place, but very close to second.

"Way to go," said Brendon after Philip joined them.

"It's yours to win," Philip answered. "Hi, Ross."

"Mr. Holmes," said Ross, giving him the nod and smile.

"Well," said Philip to Courtney and Brendon, "take it away." The two of them walked *Dues* back to the starting area. "Be aggressive!" Philip called after them.

Courtney gave the thumbs-up sign.

The twelve finalists were quickly lined up, and before Clayton could edge close enough to bait Brendon again, the starting gun fired and the sails flared.

Immediately Courtney trimmed the sail so perfectly that *Dues* began planing at close to top speed. Both Brendon and Courtney hiked out when *Dues* cleared the harbor and caught the full brunt of the wind. Suddenly, the only boat ahead of them was the Phantom that had set the pace in the first lap. And he was flying.

106

Brendon couldn't believe how good he felt, calm yet fully alert, completely involved. He handled the tiller efficiently as he gripped the gunwales for balance. They had reached top speed and seemed to be putting distance between themselves and the pack, but not gaining at all on the leader.

Brendon looked back only once on the way to Rock Island, and he was glad to see Clayton Wills fading, misreading the wind so badly his sail was barely in trim.

Soon it was time for *Dues* to come about the Rock Island buoy and make its run for home. As they neared the bouncing marker, Brendon yelled, "Ready?" Courtney nodded, and Brendon shoved the tiller away. *Dues* cut to port, the sail slapping as it dumped wind. The boom swung over their ducking heads, the Dacron bulging again as the skiff raced for the finish line on a straight, close-hauled tack.

Courtney and Brendon knew they had second place bagged and still an outside shot at first.

Suddenly Courtney hollered, "Watch out!"

Brendon followed her outstretched hand and saw that Clayton Wills had broken from the pack, cut behind the buoy, and was angling his Laser right at them, bent on a collision course.

"What's he *doing*!" hollered Brendon.

"I don't believe it."

"Trying to ram us?"

"Don't let him," said Courtney.

Brendon looked toward Jackson Harbor and the finish line, trying to see if Wills could actually cut them off. It was obvious, even to Brendon, that he might. Brendon thought about slowing a little when the boats met and letting Clayton think he could hit them, but then back-cutting him, shooting by his stern, and breaking away.

Before Brendon could communicate his plan, Wills was on top of them.

"Go for it!" screamed Courtney. "Hold steady!" Meaning try to outrun him, Brendon assumed. But he hesitated, bore off just enough to blow the slim chance they had to keep on course and miss Wills. Now Brendon had to bear hard to port to avoid a collision. The sail emptied and *Dues* floundered as Wills slowed to block them completely.

While Brendon and Courtney struggled to find a tack, Wills called out, "Hey, Slick, which way to Washington Island?"

By now half a dozen boats had rushed by them and the leader was about to finish.

Finally, they found an angle, caught the wind, and slipped past Wills. *Dues* hurried to shore in time to place a disappointing eighth. When the skiff crossed the line, Philip Holmes was fuming.

No sooner had Clayton Wills run his Laser aground than Philip was in his face, hollering and pushing his forefinger against Clayton's chest. Brendon saw Wills try to shrug it off, but Philip persisted, getting madder and madder. Brendon hurried closer.

It was when Clayton slapped Philip's hand aside and pushed him back hard, nearly knocking him down, that Brendon reacted. He stepped between Wills and Philip, crouched, and put a hard, straight left jab right on the point of Clayton's nose.

When the punch connected, Clay's mouth and eyes jumped wide open. His nose began bleeding badly. Still, he managed to lift an arm and thrust it at Brendon's head. It was not a wild blow but a fluid, well-timed punch. As Brendon ducked it, he realized Wills knew what he was doing in a fight.

Then Wills tried an uppercut that nicked Brendon, enraging him. So he slammed his left forearm across Wills's throat and buried his right fist in Clayton's gut, just below the sternum.

Clutching at his neck, his eyes bulging, Wills made a retching sound. While a crowd gathered, Clay fell to his knees, blood dripping from his nose and mouth. He bent forward and vomited. Then he lay there writhing, his eyes tightly shut.

Philip pulled Brendon aside and said, "Get up by the car." Brendon obeyed. His heart was making huge staggering beats, throbs he could feel in his throat and ears. Truman Wills was coming over.

As Brendon turned away, Clayton yelled, "Goddam blindsider!! I won't forget this, you hear?"

"Do I care?" Brendon shot back, working to maintain an outward calm while his stomach cramped and knotted itself. He looked around for Ross but couldn't find him. That made him happy. He hoped maybe Ross hadn't seen it. He hated himself for what he'd done, letting a nobody like Clayton Wills pull him into a fight. He retreated in disgrace.

Brendon found Courtney already inside the Jeep, looking plenty upset herself, staring straight ahead. She wouldn't look at him.

He'd blown it all now, he was sure of it. He'd lost the race, his temper, and probably Courtney too.

Down on the shore, Philip and Truman Wills were jawing while Clayton held his T-shirt to his bleeding face. When Philip started coming toward the Jeep, Brendon couldn't believe what he saw.

Truman Wills turned his wrath on his son. He started

hollering at him for losing the race and the fight and being so *"Pathetic!"* Clayton looked at the ground, humiliated but taking it. Brendon was embarrassed by Truman Wills and hated to see anyone shamed that way, even Clayton.

That's one thing Michael had never done, demeaned his boys in public. He'd chewed them out plenty, but always in private. He'd shown them some standards of conduct, how to deal with people and anger. And while Michael's criticism sometimes rankled Brendon, it never threatened his self-respect. Just the opposite. It made him think.

Michael had often said, "I'm telling you straight the best I know so you can make better choices, better than some of mine anyway."

Brendon doubted that Michael would respect his choices today. He'd let himself become another Clayton Wills.

"C'mon," said Philip to Brendon. "Let's pick up the boat and get out of here."

They rode home in silence.

At the cottage Brendon climbed from the Jeep. He was about to close the door, when he said, "I'm sorry. I know—"

"That's okay," said Courtney, cutting him off but facing him finally. "Maybe we can talk about it later, after I get back."

Brendon gave her a questioning look that Philip intercepted.

"We're going to the mainland for the weekend," he explained.

"Oh," said Brendon. He waited a moment to see if anyone had something to add, but all he got was silence.

Till Philip Holmes said, "I know you were only trying to help, and I appreciate that."

Brendon said, "Thanks for including me," trying now to

110

put a good face on it, but sick at heart and hating himself.

He shut the door and they left.

Inside the cottage he was greeted with, "Helluva punch, Bro."

"Helluva day," he mumbled back before disappearing into his room.

14

Helluva night, too.

Brendon didn't, *could*n't sleep.

It was a night like those *other* nights, when he was afraid to sleep. He kept his light on and tried closing his eyes, but it was no use.

Ross had said no more about the fight with Clayton. And Ross must have dropped a convincing hoax on Anne to explain Brendon's need for solitude, because she didn't look in on him either. But all evening he'd heard both of them. He knew when they got home, when they ate, when they were asleep. Finally, at dawn, Brendon dozed off for three ragged hours.

He woke up knowing he was alone.

The first thing he did was call Courtney. To apologize, again. He let the phone ring a dozen times before accepting the fact that he'd missed her. The girl was *gone*.

For most of the day, Brendon was torn between his desire to hide and his wish to look for Courtney. By late afternoon, he hadn't stepped out of the cottage and no longer planned to.

After supper, Ross came into Brendon's room and said, "He didn't show."

"Who?" Brendon asked, knowing exactly who.

"Claymore," said Ross.

"Why d'you call him that?"

"His shot," Ross explained, shaking his head. "It's like a *mine*—when he fires it off we don't know where it's going or who it's going to hit. The boy's a little erratic."

Brendon nodded, unsmiling.

"Anyway," Ross continued, "he didn't show up and it cost his three-on-three team a place in the quarterfinals. So they aren't too happy with him either."

Brendon had no interest in discussing Clayton Wills, not now.

But Anne didn't know that. Later in the evening she told Brendon, "I heard about what happened at the sailboat race."

"Who told you?"

"Beth Neal. Philip mentioned it to her."

"What'd you hear?" wondered Brendon.

"You hit a boy."

Ross said, "He's not a *boy*, Mom. He's a jerk and a cheat and a creep and . . . you want it all?"

Anne said, "I just hope he's all right."

"*He*'s all right!" blurted Brendon. "*He*'s the guy who started it, from the day we got here!"

"That's right," said Ross.

"It makes no difference," Anne replied.

"But he shoved Courtney's dad," Brendon said.

"I know that. Still, all you've done is give him a reason to cause you more trouble."

"Or *no more* trouble," remarked Ross. "Mom," he explained, "this guy's a gutless wonder from the word go, so maybe Brendon shut him down for good. Ever think of that?"

"The war to end all wars," Anne said. "Only it never works out that way."

113

Brendon could see it was hopeless to try explaining the situation further, and maybe she was right.

· · ·

Brendon stayed in for most of Saturday, too. When another call to Courtney went unanswered, he went fishing, but he couldn't concentrate well enough to forget his troubles or catch any fish.

Saturday night, with the postponed Fourth-of-July fireworks thudding dully in the distant sky, Brendon lay alone in his room, thinking. He felt himself sinking deeper into an old depression, maybe drifting in circles at best. But even those were spiraling downward.

If only he could talk to her. He didn't know what he'd say, how he could possibly explain to her what he couldn't explain to himself. But he thought that if she were there with him, and if she tried, if they were together and she helped him work through it, she might say just the right thing. For she knew much more than she'd said. And she'd been there somehow too, at the depths.

· · ·

Sunday Brendon was lost in himself and failed to see it was a gorgeous island day. Once again, Ross tried to draw him out.

"Buncha guys playing baseball this afternoon," he suggested.

"No thanks," Brendon replied.

"How about the Dunes?" said Anne, referring to Sand Dunes Park on the island's south shore. "It's perfect weather for that."

"Be too crowded," said Brendon.

"Fine," said Anne. "Suit yourself."

And that was it, the end of the overtures.

114

Late Sunday night, Brendon heard that Courtney might be back on the island Monday. Anne told him. So he'd at least have a chance to straighten things out. He would certainly explain how bad he felt at embarrassing everybody.

Just before turning in, Brendon was able to let himself off the hook a little. The others were already in bed, and he was still in the bathroom, staring at his face in the mirror, asking it what the hell was wrong with him. Why couldn't he just take care of things? That's when he thought of Wills and the race and the fight, and involuntarily he broke into a smile. A split second later he knew why—it had been just a helluva nice left jab, straight and solid, perfect form. Michael would've loved it, his execution anyway.

"There comes a time," Michael had said, "when you must fight to defend your*self*."

Maybe so, thought Brendon.

• • •

Late Monday afternoon Courtney phoned.

Brendon answered, said, "You're back."

"Yeah. And I've got lots to tell you."

"Me too," he replied. Then he asked, "Is it bad news?"

"I have to tell you," she said ambiguously.

"Same here. I—"

"Not now," she cut in. "I want to see you, okay? Tell you in person."

"Sure. When?"

"Fifteen minutes?"

"Okay."

"Fine," said Courtney, and hung up.

• • •

Courtney drove the white Jeep in, just seconds after Ross returned from a fairly successful afternoon of fishing. When

115

she came to a stop and pushed open her door, both boys were stunned. Her gold silk shorts and matching tank top looked great with her tan, her hair, her smile.

Ross started with, "Hi."

Courtney's smile shone, then flickered. "Gambini," she said, "that was a really *swell* call. Thanks a bunch."

Ross slid into a confused look, shrugged, his eyes going from Courtney to Brendon, asking What's that mean?

"The race," she said, reading *his* mind. "You called it right . . . unfortunately."

"Well yeah," Ross answered. "Sometimes it's hard to be right."

"That's a fact," said Courtney. Then turning to Brendon, she asked, "How about an ice cream cone?"

"Why not?" he answered, trying to play it slow and careful.

"How about you, Gambini? Care to join us?"

Brendon caught Ross's eye with a forbidding look, its message unmistakable.

"No, that's okay," Ross replied. "I need some rest. Omniscience is exhausting."

"I bet," said Courtney.

"So you guys just run along, have fun," said Ross. "Don't worry about me."

"Will we have fun?" Courtney asked.

Again, Ross closed his eyes tightly, pressed his fingertips to his forehead. "The odds are nine in ten," he predicted. He opened his eyes and smiled.

"Have you *ever* been wrong, Gambini?"

"Uh-uh. And you know something? My name isn't really Gambini."

"Oh, c'mon," Courtney replied as Brendon climbed into the Jeep. "Be proud . . . though maybe I'd say the same thing if my name was Gambini. It's just different, that's all." She gave Ross another big grin, waved, and drove out to West Harbor Road.

She took Brendon to a small, old-time ice cream parlor on Main Road where they each bought mammoth single-scoop chocolate chip cones. Then she drove to School House Beach.

. . .

Alone in the park, Brendon and Courtney sat on a picnic table and watched the slow, meager swells working their way in.

"Is your dad still upset?" asked Brendon.

"He was for a while."

"Because I blew it, the race."

"No, not that. Because things got out of control."

"He thinks it's my fault."

"No."

"Do you?"

She looked directly at him, her eyes probing. "Do you?" she asked.

"Uh-huh."

"It scared me," she said.

"Me too. I was afraid I might kill him."

"Don't, please."

"What?"

"Talk like that."

"I was only—"

"Could we talk about something else?" she asked.

So Brendon tried, "I haven't asked Gambini what you did on the mainland, in case you're worried."

"I am. I admit it." She turned to him, gave a big mock sigh of relief.

"Worried about what he heard? Or what you did."

"It could easily be misinterpreted," she answered.

"So you've decided to give me your version first."

"Well, since you're going to find out anyway, sooner or later, I suppose that'd be best, don't you?"

Brendon nodded. But he wasn't sure where the kidding stopped and the truth started. He offered her a brittle smile. "So what happened?" he asked.

"I was with some friends from home," she said quietly. "Generally, that sums it up. A whole bunch of friends, about ten more than I expected to see. And they all just happened to know somebody else up here so the party schedule grew and grew."

"Any old boyfriends?"

"Any old one'll do fine," she countered.

"Sorry."

"Actually, there was, but he went home. We somehow continued without him."

"Wild affairs?" said Brendon. "Reckless indulgence?"

"I was a slave to impulse, what else."

"Drug abuse? Satanic music?"

"It's a fast crowd. Should I really tell all?" She smiled coyly.

"Start with pharmaceuticals," said Brendon, trying to sound detached. Meanwhile his heart hammered against his ribs. What were the limits? he wondered.

"There was a little of this and a little of that in a lot of places. We've been through something this year, my friends. Something we're trying to forget."

Brendon waited for more, but Courtney didn't elaborate. He wanted to ask her about her own habits. But he didn't dare; it would be so immature.

"You're wondering about me, right?"

118

"I guess. Sure," he said.

"Okay. Officially, for the record, and Gambini will back me on this, I can be around it, okay? I have been for years, haven't I. With Philip, I mean. It bothers me a lot. Personally, I need a clear head. I don't want to miss *anything*."

Brendon nodded.

"You understand that, don't you?"

"I think so," he said.

"You know what I think?" she asked.

He shook his head, then licked his cone.

"I think you missed me."

He nodded. "I did."

"Which brings us right to the point. You're famous over there."

"Really? How?"

"You'll never guess who pushed his way into most of the bigger parties."

"Who?"

"Your not-so-friendly rival, Clayton Wills."

Brendon sneered automatically, then tried to hide it without much success.

"He doesn't give up, that boy," Courtney continued. "I never had to use my ditsy voice for so long without a rest. You should see what you did to him."

"How bad did he look?"

"*Baaaaaad.* His nose was taped and his eyes were black, and all the time he wore these ugly wraparound sunglasses, day and night. Everybody thought he was some big doper."

"He is."

"Anyhow, I told him you were kind of crazy and to stay away from you. Told him you suffered from an acute Ulysses complex."

119

Brendon smiled. "What'd he say?"

"Can I show you?" She climbed off the picnic table and started for the Jeep.

"I don't get it," said Brendon.

Courtney pulled an envelope from her purse. "Look at this," she said.

"What is it?"

"A letter I wrote you that turned out to be a story."

Brendon asked, "What kind of story?"

"Fantasy mostly. Maybe allegory. Here, you read it and tell me what you think. It was fun to do, I'll say that. Helped me stay in character." She opened the envelope and offered him several handwritten pages. "I missed you too," she added.

Brendon gave her a guarded smile and took the letter. He glanced at it and saw she'd written it in Bimbo Script—there were little circles dotting the *i*'s and forests of exclamation marks after every other sentence. He read:

MISSING U.

When the Venus Summer League announced the dates of its weekend-long Peninsula Party, all of the vacationing nymphs, including yours truly, were like really excited!! The Party only comes once a year and it's the only opportunity some of us have to show off like our taste in summer fashion and which gods and heroes we know and who our totally gnarly foxy date is!!

Okay, so like there was my big problem. Who can I ask? He had to be a super hunk or I would like die of embarrassment!!!! Well, I'd just met this one guy who was like unparalleled. What a bod! What a head!! I'm talking about Ulysses, of course, my island bud.

So anyway, things were like working out just the

120

way I'd planned. One day we wound up in just the right place and in just the right mood, you know? But like when it came time for me to Pop The Question, I like choked! I mean, I couldn't go for it, you know?! Wasted so much time getting up my nerve that pretty soon it was . . . TOO LATE!!!!!!

So with U. off on the island, like what was I supposed to do? Hang upside down in a dark closet all weekend? I'm so sure!! Like GO! GO! GO!! I told myself. Of course, I'd miss being with U., but like I thought Nymph babble at the Peninsula Party Weekend was better than no P.P.W. at all. I mean really!!

So, okay, there I was, at the big opener, a Poolside Pageant at Nymph Crissy's place. Her parents' place, actually. Anyway, Crissy even had a live band called Saturnalia to keep things loose. I was like just getting into a good mood, laughing it up with The Nymphs, when who should come stumbling up to me but Cy-CLAYps. That's right, Cy-CLAYps of NO-MIND!!

Right away I could tell he was like pretty wasted, and he was wearing these really weird sunglasses. I tried to ignore him, but that doesn't work with Cy. No way!! At parties, he goes for whatever he wants.

So then he like taps (slaps) me on the shoulder and says, "Look who's here."

So I scope the place and say, "Who?"

"You, nymph," he says. "And ME!"

"So?"

"Opens up some possibilities, huh," he says, really mush-mouthed, you know, so right away I'm sure he's been with Bacchus again. Old Cy can smell free spirits an ocean away. I mean really!! And now, I thought, he's after yours truly!

He kept hanging around so I asked, "Like where are your eyes, dude? I mean it's eleven P.M.!!" That was the exact wrong thing to say. Like it was supposed to be a put-down, you know? But it was really the opening he wanted.

"Ask your tricky little playmate, Ulysses," he says.

So okay, then he starts telling me this story about how U. "sucker punched" him, and for effect Cy whips off his weird sunglasses and shows me his WOUNDS!!

"How rude!!" I said. "Gross me out to the max!!!!" I mean his eyes were red and black where they should have been white! And like his nose was turning BLUE!!

So then he puts on this little pout, like I'm supposed to feel sorry for him or something?! I'm so sure!!!

"So like what else is new?" I ask.

For a second he doesn't know what to say, then he goes, "You wanna have some fun?" He puts on his glasses again.

I said, "In a sec. I mean like right now I gotta call my broker, you know?"

So I tried to walk away from him fast but like there was Crissy. You know, my hostess? I mean right behind me!!!

"So who's the wildman partyer?" she whispers to me, looking over my shoulder at Cy-CLAYps, who's slouching against the wall, like trying to stay on his feet!!

"Like you don't know?!" I said, faking astonishment.

"Wish I did!!" she says.

I go, "Un-REAL!! Nymph, you're in luck!" So I turn around to make introductions but before I can get to it Crissy like grabs my arm and whispers, "He's cute but is he, you know, fun?"

"He's capital F-U-N!!" I said. "But like he's not too bright, you know?"

122

"Hey, do I care what goes on above the neck at P.P.W.?!!" says Crissy. "I'm so sure!!! I mean, grow up, nymph!!"

So I got them together and Cy liked her so they started trading lies almost before I could leave.

After that—like for the next THREE DAYS!!—whenever I saw Crissy alone she would go on and on about how much she liked Cy, how totally massive he was, what a crazy date and all that.

"He only has one hang-up," says Crissy. "I mean he REALLY wants to get this guy Ulysses. He says that if he can't do it, his daddy will."

"Like who's his daddy?" I ask.

"You mean you don't know NEPTUNE?!? I'm so sure!!! I mean, c'mon nymph, get with it! He's big around here!!"

But by then like I'd lost interest in Cy and Crissy and Daddy Nep and all the rest of 'em. P.P.W. was like losing its charm, you know? Wearing really thin.

"Here's to Missing U.," I said each night before downing my ritual glass of ginger ale. "Here's to Missing U. . . ."

As he read the story, Brendon chuckled and snickered almost continuously.

"This is great," he said softly, starting to reread it.

"You think so?"

Brendon nodded. "Great."

"It just shows you," said Courtney.

"What?" Brendon said, looking up.

"If I write to you next year, you might enjoy it."

"The ultimate pen pal," concluded Brendon. "I won't write back, though."

"Why not?" A hurt look crossed her face.

"Can't top this, no way."

"It just shows you."

. . .

As they rode back to West Harbor, Brendon realized that Courtney was exhausted. Still, she asked, "Want to sail *Dues* tomorrow?"

"Sure."

"I'll call you when I wake up . . . if I wake up." She stifled a yawn and drove out.

And Brendon stood there thinking maybe he'd have his second chance.

15

They didn't sail again until Thursday. The island weather, ever changing, turned cloudy and cool until late Wednesday afternoon.

Aside from two phone calls, Brendon had had no time with Courtney. She used all of Tuesday to rest and recover from her exciting, sleepless weekend. On Wednesday, Philip took her to an all-day barbecue and fish boil on the east side of the island.

Thursday morning she called to say, "I'm ready for our sailing date."

"It's okay with your dad?"

"I told you he's over it, the race. He *likes* you. Why can't you believe that?"

Brendon replied, "I wanted to be sure it's okay."

"You can never be *sure*," she said. "Not with Philip. It's a day-to-day thing, remember?"

"Uh-huh."

"But today's all right. We have his *blessing*."

There it was again, thought Brendon. That odd tone, a disturbing mixture of sarcasm and affection. Did she know how she sounded? Did she really know how she felt about her father? Did he, about his?

By the time Brendon arrived at the cabin, Philip Holmes had left to "meet some people." Courtney had *Dues* rigged and ready.

"Great conditions," she said as they walked down to the dock. "Steady northeast wind."

So they took *Dues* on a straight tack right to the edge of Figenschau Bay, where the Little Islands formed the natural western breakwater.

"Let's keep going," said Brendon.

"Where?"

"Past the islands, into the open."

"You serious?"

"Sure."

". . . Okay."

So he steered for the headwaters of Green Bay, and it wasn't long before Brendon felt a powerful surge that far outsized anything they'd encountered during the Channel Challenge race. Each huge, slow-moving swell lifted *Dues* high on a crest before rushing it down to the trough. For Brendon it was both fascinating and frightening, being caught up in such a force while being part of it too.

"You feel that?" Brendon asked, excited.

"The waves?"

"What's in them."

"It's dangerous," she said.

He knew he was enjoying the thrill of breaking for big water, and *Dues* seemed to be weathering the challenge fairly well. They passed a thirty-five-foot Morgan sloop heading for Detroit Harbor, and some people on deck waved, clapped, and called out, "Pretty gutsy!"

Brendon smiled and waved back, holding his course.

126

But Courtney ended it, snapped the mood by saying, "We better turn around, okay? We're a long way out."

For the first time Brendon looked back. He couldn't believe the distance they'd covered.

"All right," he said, and they prepared to come about.

During the trip back, as they neared the Little Islands, they heard a whining engine getting closer. It seemed to be bearing down on them from the south, coming straight at them. Brendon watched helplessly while the sleek sixteen-foot silver-flecked runabout roared in. As it cut the distance, it unleashed all its hundred horses of power.

"Whatever you do, hang on," said Brendon.

When the runabout came within ten feet of them, its bow high in the water, the driver hit the air horn and veered sharply, sending a huge, walling wake at them. It slammed them broadside, drenching them, and knocking them halfway out of the boat. *Dues* nearly rolled.

"Dammit!" yelled Brendon.

Courtney could only grunt as she coughed for air and pushed her wet curls from her eyes.

They'd both seen him clearly, grinning maliciously behind the wheel with his hand on the throttle. He was still wearing his unmistakable wraparound sunglasses.

"Look!" said Brendon, as he frantically bailed the cockpit with cupped hands.

They watched with anger and dread as the runabout made a wide arcing turn and started at them again for a second strafing.

"Quick," hollered Brendon. "When I get the wind, keep it close-hauled."

With the sail full, the mast straining, the skiff heeling dangerously, Brendon pointed *Dues* right at Clayton Wills. The two boats charged each other, Clayton's outboard coming at five times the speed of *Dues*.

Brendon was within striking distance sooner than he expected. Just as Wills began his veer move, cutting even closer this time, Brendon signaled Courtney to release the mainsheet. He watched as the fourteen-foot lower spar whipped out and smashed into the fiberglass hull of Wills's boat, punching a small ragged hole in it.

The impact jarred the mast, sending a concussion through *Dues*. Brendon fell overboard. Only his grip on the tiller kept him from losing *Dues* altogether. Courtney had managed to grab the mast with both hands. By the time Brendon was back on board, Wills had gone a hundred yards north of them. He set the idle and hung himself over the side to inspect the damage.

When Clayton spotted the hole, he stood up in the cockpit and looked back at *Dues*. Brendon and Courtney returned his stare. Moments passed. Brendon was trying to think of another tactic should Clayton mount a third attack.

Finally, Wills dropped back down in the pilot's chair, slammed the throttle forward to full power, and raced off. This time, though, he ran north and disappeared around the first jutting bluff.

Brendon hoped he was taking the long way home, buying time to dream up an explanation for Daddy Truman, who didn't seem likely to accept excuses. Who would no doubt deal with Clayton the same way Clayton was trying to handle Brendon. You don't have to look too hard at a guy, thought Brendon, to see his father staring back at you.

"He could've killed us," said Courtney.

"I think he wants to."

"No kidding?"

"He's not kidding."

"Will he come back?"

"Hope not," Brendon said, struggling to curb his rage.

"He doesn't want us to sail," said Courtney.

"He doesn't want us together."

"I just thought of something *really* sick."

"Yeah? What's that?"

"Maybe he *likes* Bimbo. Maybe she's exactly what he wants, you know?"

"Something to think about."

Courtney looked off, puzzled. "How *could* he?" she asked herself.

"C'mon," said Brendon. "Let's go home."

But Brendon was even more upset with Wills when they reached shore. Clayton had stolen something from him *again*—the good feelings that came from sailing well and being with Courtney.

16

When Brendon called Courtney on Friday he learned that some of her mainland friends had surprised her with a visit.

"You can meet them," she suggested. "They know all about you, a few things anyway."

"Maybe," Brendon answered, suddenly wary.

"Want the schedule?" she asked.

"Which one?"

"My events calendar. So our paths can cross," she explained.

"You told Wills about any of this?"

"No. C'mon."

"Good. I ever *see* him again . . ."

"Forget it."

"His girl Crissy come along?"

"Uh-uh."

Brendon waited for a few seconds. "Okay," he said, "I'm ready."

So Courtney listed all the activities she wanted to crowd into her three-day weekend with friends. That afternoon and evening it was a boat ride around the island with some friend of Philip's. Later, the girls were supposed to visit someone's aunt and uncle. Saturday, the father of another good friend was picking them up with his twenty-eight-foot Bristol yacht and sailing them around the outer islands. They'd anchor somewhere for lunch and a swim.

On Sunday was a baseball game, and even more of the mainland crowd would be there.

"So whadaya say?" asked Courtney. "Any possibilities?"

"A few," Brendon replied, thinking, very few.

"Which?"

"We probably won't meet Saturday, on the high seas."

She laughed. "Probably not."

"The ball game, I suppose."

"Not before?"

"I don't know."

"What if we stop by your place? Will you come out and say Hi?"

"Uh-huh."

"Okay. That's a start."

"Have fun," said Brendon.

• • •

Courtney and her friends didn't stop at Brendon's, and Brendon didn't see her or them until Sunday. He decided to go to the baseball game, rather than add to his reputation as Social Cretin. So following a leisurely morning with the *Chicago Tribune*, Brendon rode his bike to the ball field.

When he arrived he discovered a big crowd, a rare find on the island. Cars were parked haphazardly all along both shoulders of Main Road. The game was already in progress, Washington Island versus Sister Bay. Brendon pulled in to look for Courtney.

He walked his bike through the parking area, chained it to a tree, and headed for the bleachers behind the home plate backstop. He saw the Washington Island pitcher deliver a called third strike to an irate Sister Bay batter. The out ended the inning. While the teams changed places, Brendon looked around for the scoreboard and Courtney. He spotted both above the crowd packed in along a snow fence running down the first baseline.

Courtney was bunched with eight or ten other high school kids in the bed of an old pickup truck that had been backed to the fence. The group was having a high old time taunting the Sister Bay first baseman.

Brendon watched as two of the guys knelt over a cooler, sneaking cans of beer into the Pepsi cups being passed around the group. He saw Courtney holding one. She took a sip and handed it to the guy next to her. Brendon stood a second more, debating whether or not to go further.

But before he could decide, Clayton Wills, wearing his wraparound sunglasses, cut between Brendon and Courtney. He approached the truck and tried to climb in. Some of the others made halfhearted efforts to keep him from joining them. Someone even poured beer on his head before hauling him up.

Then another tall, swarthy guy clad only in wildly striped swimming trunks threw an arm around Courtney and pulled her to him. She laughed and made a token struggle to get away. Brendon held his ground. Then she caught him staring. She shrugged out of the swarthy boy's grip and waved Brendon over.

Instead of waving back, Brendon turned around and walked away. He felt completely unsure of who Courtney was and what he meant to her. Was he just another guy in her life, one of *many*? Had they really shared anything special?

Aboard his ten-speed, back on Main Road, Brendon raced north determined to lap the island until he was exhausted, empty. But it didn't work. When he had torn all the way around and was nearing home, he realized that once again he had tried to solve a problem with action, but not the kind that brought progress. This time he was literally going in circles.

That night Courtney called him.

"I saw you at the game," she said.

"I know."

"What are you, bashful? I never would've guessed. Why didn't you come over?"

"You looked too busy."

"Yeah. We were having fun. The Islanders lost, though."

"Hm."

"Those guys I was with?"

"Uh-huh?"

"They're from my high school."

"I thought so."

A silence settled on the conversation.

Courtney broke it. "Brendon, is something wrong?"

"You," he said bluntly. "I don't know what you want from me."

There was another pause.

Courtney said, "I like you, spending time with you. It's been really nice."

Brendon's heart began hammering. "I can't afford it," he said.

"What's that mean?"

"Things have gotten too complicated."

Again she waited before responding. "Are you mad about

the game?" she asked. "The boy with me when I saw you?"

"Look, I don't want to get into—"

"Tell me," she said firmly.

"That your real boyfriend?" he asked.

". . . Listen," she said, "we have to talk, okay? Alone, face-to-face. There's something you should know about."

But Brendon felt unwilling to risk a confrontation.

"Can you come over? Philip is gone."

"I can't see—"

"Please," she said. "It's important. I don't want you to misunderstand."

"Misunderstand what?"

"I'll tell you."

So Brendon agreed to ride to Courtney's one more time. It was late, past sunset, but neither Anne nor Ross commented when Brendon said he was going out for a while.

Racing his bike down West Harbor Road, Brendon discovered that the night was surprisingly warm, the soft breeze on his face helping to calm him. He would hear her out, then gracefully retreat, be smarter next time.

When he knocked at the cabin door, she answered quickly, said, "It's hot inside. Let's go by the water."

Brendon nodded and followed her down to the dock where *Dues* was tied. They sat on a little bench and looked out over Figenschau Bay. The moonlight made a silvery track on the moving water.

"You ready?" asked Courtney.

"For what?"

"I want to tell you about something that happened this last year, something all of us are still trying to deal with."

"All your friends?"

"The kids at the game, on the mainland."

"Okay."

"Well . . . in March . . ."

Brendon gazed at Courtney's eyes, found them glistening, infinitely sad. "What happened?" he asked.

"This boy we all knew, the captain of the basketball team, Jay Vaughn . . . in March he killed himself." She stared back at Brendon, watching for his reaction.

He looked down. Finally he managed to ask, "Why?"

"Why'd he do it?"

Brendon nodded.

"That's what's hard. Nobody knows, really. He had lots of friends, he was doing okay in school, the team made it to region finals. Then one night I got this call from Laurie. She's one of the girls who stayed here," Courtney explained. "Jay was her boyfriend."

Brendon was speechless. He'd never known anybody who'd committed suicide. He'd never even talked to friends of someone who had. "I don't know what to say."

"Nobody does. Nobody did. You should've seen it, the whole school just stopped, even the teachers. Everyone was in shock for a week. There were five hundred people at the funeral, and another couple hundred outside who couldn't get in."

"What a waste," Brendon said.

"And Laurie, she came into the church with Jay's parents, like the grieving widow or something. And she stayed with that all spring, crying all the time, missing lots of classes. We didn't know how to help. She's just coming out of it now."

"Which one was she?" Brendon asked, feeling a sudden closeness with Laurie.

"She's really pretty, dark hair and brown eyes. She was right next to me at the game."

Brendon tried to remember the crowd, but couldn't find Laurie.

"You see her?" asked Courtney.

Brendon shook his head. "I guess not."

"All of us were goners till school ended. There was even a time when everyone hated Jay for what he did."

"Why?"

"Well here was this boy who had lots and lots of friends, who was famous even, but did he ask anybody for help? Did he ever try to share anything, get some perspective?"

"He didn't?"

"No. Just the opposite. He used his friends to help him do it."

"I don't understand."

"That guy you saw me with, his arm around me?"

"Yeah."

"I once went out with him, but that's not important. He was Jay's best friend, and on the night Jay died Tom called Jay's parents and told them Jay was staying with him. Jay had talked him into lying. Tom thought Jay had a hot date or something."

"You?"

"No," she answered coldly.

"Sorry, I didn't mean—"

"Try to *see* it, okay?"

Brendon was startled by her pleading yet commanding tone. "I'll try," he said.

"So Jay had it all planned out. And he used Tom, and then left him behind to blame himself."

"Where was he when he . . . you know . . ."

"Inside the garage of an empty house. Shut the door, start the car, and goodbye."

"He leave a note?"

"Uh-huh. And all it said was he felt really really tired and had to get some rest."

Brendon waited, but Courtney had stopped talking. "That was it?" he asked.

"Yes," said Courtney. "I'll never forget what one of the counselors said later. She said Jay seemed like the kind of person that if he would've talked things out with someone, he'd still be alive."

Brendon shook his head slowly.

"But look what he did instead, what he did to us."

"What?" asked Brendon.

"He as much as said you guys aren't worth waiting around for. And we thought we knew him."

That comment stunned Brendon. It was exactly the way he felt about Michael sometimes. His father was someone whose image they relied on and believed in, yet he virtually committed suicide by driving his Death Car that night. And Brendon hadn't stopped him.

"Why didn't you tell me this before?" asked Brendon.

"You mean like after you told me about your dad?"

"Then, sure."

"I thought about it. I was going to. But I didn't want you to think I was just trading stories or something."

"I wouldn't have thought that."

"I know," she said, "now. But there was something else."

"What?"

"I saw a lot of Jay. And you're like him."

137

"How?"

"Trying to deal with something big all by yourself."

Brendon didn't know what to say.

"Nothing like this ever happened to me," said Courtney. "To any of us, and we'd be even worse off if we didn't have each other. Tom is still real shaky, he feels so bad. He drinks too much, and has to see a psychiatrist."

Brendon said, "He can't let himself off the hook."

"No."

"Don't," said Brendon.

"Don't what?"

"Ever forget. Think about it, make yourself look straight at it till you understand. Otherwise you'll never be off the hook."

"Are you off the hook?" she asked.

"No. Not yet."

"Why?"

"Because I can't *do* anything about it now, change what happened, what we were."

"You and your dad?"

Brendon gave a quick nod.

"I thought you got along."

"Sort of. But not like my brother."

"If there's nothing you can do, why worry about it?"

"Why do you worry? About this Jay, I mean?"

"He won't leave us alone."

"Exactly," said Brendon. "I want my dad off my back too."

Courtney remained silent.

"Look," said Brendon, standing up and rubbing his hands nervously, "could we go someplace? Move around a little?"

"Where?"

"I don't know. Someplace."

138

"Take a walk?"

"No, I mean *go* someplace." Then looking at *Dues*, Brendon said, "How about that?"

"It's too dark."

"No it isn't. There's a moon."

Courtney looked over the bay, but said, "Philip wouldn't like it."

"So?"

Courtney scanned the black shoreline, said, "So you want to kill yourself too?"

Brendon said, "I want to go out there as far as I can and *live*, feel something."

Courtney turned that over for a moment before saying, "Then I'll have to go with you."

So they donned life jackets, rigged *Dues*, and pushed off. They were lucky and caught enough of a breeze to pull the boat out of the annoying little waves sloshing around the dock pilings. Courtney slid down the oversized centerboard, took up the mainsheet, and trimmed the sail. They sliced across the bay, heading straight for the Little Islands.

As they neared the mouth of the bay, Brendon said, "Let's take it out a ways." He recalled the thrill of the big swells.

"C'mon, Brendon," said Courtney. "That's too dangerous. Let's stay close to shore."

But Brendon didn't change his course. "Just a quick look," he said. By now they were passing the Little Islands and entering Green Bay. Brendon smelled the lake wind and watched the green-black roll of the mild swells, felt them grab the skiff and begin pushing it along. The power had found them. And they went with it.

After cruising awhile longer, Courtney said, "Look over there."

Squinting, Brendon spotted the glimmer on little Pilot Island. "A lighthouse," he said. Then he stared at the scattered twinkling far off on the mainland.

They surged easily along on the gathering swells for another few minutes before Courtney said, "This is far enough. We've got to turn back right now."

"We can make it," said Brendon.

"Make what?"

"Cross the Door," he said just as the idea crossed his mind.

"Are you *crazy*?!" Courtney shrieked, plainly scared. "Turn this damn thing around!" she hollered, letting the sail out.

"We'll be halfway pretty soon. We can go over and back tonight, no sweat."

"Brendon, I don't want to. *Please*."

But Brendon didn't hear.

17

"Ever heard of Gerry Spiess?" Brendon asked while *Dues* held its course for the mainland.

Resigned, Courtney said nothing, but kept the sail in trim.

"He's from Minneapolis," Brendon went on. "And a few years ago he sailed across the Atlantic from west to east in a ten-foot homemade boat, the *Yankee Girl.*"

Again, Brendon's words were met with stony silence.

"You hear me?" asked Brendon. "He crossed the Atlantic Ocean in a boat two feet *shorter* than *Dues.* So we can handle it, okay? We're almost there. This is one we can win."

"So *that's* it!" said Courtney. "The Channel Challenge, you want to make up for losing."

"I don't know."

"What then?"

"I'm not sure yet."

"Oh that's great," she said. "Wonderful. Let me know when you figure out why I'm risking my life." She tightened her grip on the gunwales, the mainsheet.

"We'll be okay," assured Brendon. But just as he finished, far-off thunder rumbled in the west. They both saw lightning in the distance, then felt the warm gusts of a storm wind.

"*No,*" Brendon whispered.

141

"Let's open it up!" yelled Courtney. "We gotta *move*!!"

She adjusted the sail and the boat began to cut the edge, pick up speed. Brendon watched the thin gray clouds streaming over the moon, just ahead of the pitch black storm line.

They couldn't seem to make *Dues* go fast enough. They didn't appear to be getting any closer to the mainland.

Brendon's heart was pounding furiously and he struggled to control his breathing. He couldn't let Courtney see that he was losing his nerve.

Then, without warning, almost soundlessly, a vicious gust tore into the sail, ripping the mainsheet from Courtney's hand, burning her fingers.

She caught the end of it but not in time to keep the boom from gybing. Courtney shrieked and ducked as the spar whipped by overhead, missing them both by inches. Brendon saw that her eyes were wide and blank.

Before either of them could speak, even to curse, a barrage of thunder cracked almost directly above them and white beams of lightning flashed everywhere. The mast writhed in the wind.

Crouching low, her face and chest flush with the deck and her fingers tightly curled around the gunwales, Courtney pulled in the mainsheet.

"Hang on!" Brendon yelled. He couldn't believe how quickly things had changed. He was scared to imagine how bad they might get.

The thunder and lightning were now simultaneous. The first drops of rain splattered down, dimpling the water. The swells began rising into breakers, first three then six feet, trough to crest. Sometimes the whitecaps broke against the boat, sending spray across their faces. Other times *Dues*

142

became a surfboard riding out a curl. Now Brendon's greatest fear was that a comber would catch them from behind and somersault the skiff.

The rain rapidly became so heavy Brendon could no longer see the lights on the mainland. The wind had turned cold and began to tear at them, gnawing their arms and faces, pulling tears from their eyes. Their clothes were soaked. Their teeth chattered.

Brendon's arm muscles bulged as he fought to control the boat, and his heart raced with the fear that *Dues* might break up any second. Soon he was pounded numb by the ceaseless rain.

Then came the worst of it. The boat got caught in a big following wave and nose-dived. Water came slamming over the deck.

Brendon heard Courtney scream just as the mainsheet went slack. Squinting and moaning to himself, he grabbed for her, felt her jacket, and held on. She was still aboard.

"The mast!" she yelled. "Help me!"

With one hand Brendon tried to keep the tiller straight and avoid going broadside and logrolling the skiff. With the other hand he reached for the mast. It was bent, knocked at a right angle where it entered the step. The sail was half in, half out of the water. It dragged the boat, threatened to pull it sideways. The oversized centerboard, the weakened mast. "No, no, *no*!" he muttered. The crash with Wills—did that flaw the mast? Did it matter now?

"We have to change places!" he hollered over the thunder.

At first Courtney shook her head violently, too afraid to release the solid grip she had.

"C'mon!" he shouted. "You gotta do it! I have to pull the mast out and break it!"

When the wind dropped for a minute, they tried moving. They scrambled around each other. Brendon jerked the mast up in the step and bent the aluminum pipe over far enough to snap off the short end piece. He pulled the stub from the deck. But the new base end was pinched, perhaps so much it wouldn't fit back in the opening. His shot had to be perfect.

Brendon yanked up the mast, let out a yell, and speared the jagged end into the step hole. By splintering the frame, he managed to get the pipe driven in a few inches. The sail ballooned and *Dues* raced on.

Then a slashing gust hit the boat and it surged wildly. The bow plunged again. Brendon had been caught too far forward. Next a huge wave broke across the boat, knocking Brendon overboard.

The only things that saved him were his preserver and Courtney's screams. He lunged for her cries and caught the rudder.

"Slide up!" he yelled as the boat dragged him along.

Instead of following orders, she turned around and grabbed his arms, pulling him half on board before she ran out of room in the cockpit. He crawled up the rest of the way as she crouched again and fumbled for the mainsheet.

They had no idea how far they'd gone or what direction they were going until a wall of water lifted and dropped them, crashing down, on a long shelf of rock. The centerboard snapped, the hull crunched with the impact. The next wave heaved them into the trees.

Screaming for joy, they scrambled out of the boat and tried to get footholds on the stark bluff. Hanging on to the bowline, Brendon tugged. He thought he knew where they were. He looked up at the sheer limestone cliff above them. The hardy cedar trees growing at bizarre angles from the cracks and fissures were all that kept Brendon and Courtney from being pulled back into the water.

Brendon grunted, still trying to drag the boat to safety.

"Let it go!" hollered Courtney through the downpour.

"No! We can't!"

With that, Courtney joined Brendon on the bowline, and together they slid the hull completely out of the water and onto a wide ledge. The rain kept hammering down on them. They had to find cover.

Feeling his way along the cliff face by gripping exposed roots and saplings, Brendon searched for an opening. Courtney hung on to the back of his jacket. After another agonizing five minutes, he found what he wanted—steps, a wooden catwalk leading up to a plateau. At the back edge of the open area was a shed. Or was it an old outhouse? At this point Brendon didn't much care.

He pulled the rickety door open and looked inside. It was gray-black, musty, and damp. But it wasn't wet. The roof didn't leak. Brendon smelled gasoline. An equipment shed.

"Thank God," said Courtney as they ducked inside.

Once they were out of the rain, they took off their sopping life jackets. Then both broke down, crying silently. They held each other and shivered. Brendon got up, rummaged around, and discovered a tarp piled in the corner. He pulled it up, shook it out, and brought it to Courtney. "Here," he said, putting it around her shoulders. "I'm sorry. I nearly killed—"

"But you didn't," she interrupted.

Brendon sat down and said nothing.

Courtney said, "I was never so scared."

"Me either," said Brendon, even though he felt strangely euphoric too. "Thanks for yelling," he said. "I couldn't see a thing."

"We're in trouble," she said.

"We're safe."

They sat quietly for a few minutes, trying to get warm.

Then Courtney said, "You know what?"

"What?"

"When I was helping, when you were getting back on board, we connected."

"I know," said Brendon. "I felt it too. We were strong." They'd shared the thrill, Brendon realized. It wasn't just his feeling.

"We were something," she said.

"We won this time. I didn't back off and blow it for us."

"Channel Challenge II," she said, trying to laugh but coughing instead.

Brendon hugged her and said, "I suppose."

"You gotta believe now, Brendon," she said.

"Believe what?"

"There's something that makes it all worthwhile, all the trouble we've had."

"Like what?"

"Well, you can believe in yourself."

"I don't know."

"You *can*."

"You too," he said. "You're incredible. You were really good out there, really tough."

"We were better than we should've been. We played a little over our heads."

"High Times," said Brendon, thinking of his father and what he'd say about the crossing . . . if he were still alive.

"Brendon, where are you?"

"Huh?"

146

"I asked what you're thinking."

"About my dad."

"So was I."

"Philip."

"Uh-huh."

Brendon said, "I just realized how much I'm like my dad. I never saw it before."

"How like him?"

"His crazy side, the part I hated, what killed him. I mean the guy was so disciplined all the time, but then he'd do something reckless and selfish, like go rent a motorcycle and race it in the country. Once he even went skydiving without telling any of us. Then he drove himself right into an ice storm."

"That's like Philip, the writing and drinking."

"The contradictions," said Brendon.

"I used to think maybe that was it," said Courtney. "He's a bunch of contradictions and that's all, nothing solid and true about him."

"But he's different now."

"I'm still not sure."

"You said what it'll take."

"I did?"

"Believe in yourself. Then maybe you can be strong enough to accept him."

"I wonder what *they're* thinking right now," said Courtney, "Philip and your mom."

". . . We are crazy," said Brendon.

"For doing this."

"Yes."

"We're only human," she said, shivering still more.

"You all right?" he asked. "Maybe we should look for a house. Nobody would turn us away."

"If it was any colder . . ."

"We did make it," Brendon whispered.

"Absolutely."

"I mean, we're okay. We belong."

"Uh-huh."

Facing her squarely, Brendon said, "I like you. Better than anybody I've ever known." There now, it was *all* out in the open.

She looked at him and brought her face close to his. "I like you too," she said.

"I mean I *really* like you."

She said nothing more, but slid her other arm around him. They held each other that way for several moments, not kissing, just hugging each other fiercely.

• • •

They awoke at first light. They were stiff and cold. Courtney looked colorless and drawn. Brendon's right arm ached. His eyes felt grainy from sleeplessness. Their clothing was still damp.

Brendon stood up and shouldered the door all the way open. They watched as a gray morning broke over the gunmetal water of Death's Door Strait.

Next, they walked over to the edge of the bluff and looked down. There, twenty feet below them, still wedged against the cliff in a cage of cedar trees, was *Dues*.

18

"That was not only a stupid thing to do!" hollered Philip Holmes. "It was an incredibly *imbecilic* stupid thing to do!"

The three of them, with Brendon in the back, sat tightly in the chilly Jeep, waiting to board the ferry to the island.

"You hear me?"

Brendon glanced up and saw Philip looking over his shoulder, past Courtney, staring at him. He gave Philip a small nod and returned to watching the floor. Brendon shivered.

"What the hell were you thinking of?"

"I—"

"NO!" interrupted Philip. "No, don't say anything. You weren't thinking, at all! That's the point, right? Don't answer," Philip added.

Brendon had no idea what Philip wanted from him. He had tried to listen. But he couldn't do it. To Brendon, Philip and his anger seemed vague and remote. His words didn't upset Brendon. Brendon didn't feel stupid or foolish or irresponsible. He felt strong and confident. He'd had this thing to do and he'd done it.

Brendon leaned back, closed his eyes, and reviewed the morning. He and Courtney had pushed *Dues* back into the water and walked it down the shore. They'd been shocked to

149

discover that only two hundred yards from where they landed was a harmless pebble beach.

From there, they looked inland and saw a large, sprawling single-story house hidden in the hardwoods. Brendon figured the equipment shed belonged to this home. Down the coast, they spotted the Northport dock.

Rather than seek help at the house, Brendon and Courtney had decided to pull *Dues* along the shoreline, tow it to Northport. As they trudged, Brendon was angry their luck hadn't been even better. Why hadn't they landed on the beach in the first place? But he cringed when he saw just how close they'd come to missing the mainland altogether, to getting blown out on Lake Michigan. Fixing the sail had made the difference.

When they arrived at Northport, Courtney called home for help. Philip answered, told her he'd be on the next ferry.

At first Philip had been too upset to say anything. He'd simply jumped out of his Jeep and stood before them, hands on his hips, snapping his gaze from *Dues* to Brendon back to *Dues* to Courtney to Brendon . . . until Brendon broke the silence by offering to fix the sailboat. "I can do it," he'd said.

That comment sent Philip's glowering eyes back to his little homemade skiff. For the first time, he seemed to notice the broken mast and splintered topsides. He turned toward Brendon. "I don't *believe* it!" he shouted. Then he faced Courtney and asked, "Are you all right?"

Courtney nodded and hugged herself.

"You?" he asked Brendon.

"Cold."

"*Geez*," mumbled Philip, turning away. "Give me a hand," he said to Brendon.

150

The two of them loaded what was left of *Dues* onto the roof rack, tying the hull securely from several angles. Then Philip drove the Jeep back on the asphalt leading to the ferry dock. They'd been unable to get a return trip aboard the boat that brought Philip.

• • •

Finally, twenty long minutes later, another ferry appeared and they were soon on their way out to the island. Anne and Ross were waiting for them at Detroit Harbor.

After Philip had carefully guided the CJ down the steep exit ramp, he pulled up near Anne. Brendon climbed out, walked around the front of the Jeep, and faced his mother. Obviously, she hadn't slept. Her eyes were puffy, red-rimmed, and glazed.

Staring at him without blinking, she asked, "Why did you do this senseless thing?" She let her words out slowly, one at a time. Brendon knew she was struggling to hold in her anger.

"I don't know how to say it so you'll understand," he answered truthfully.

Anne continued staring at him.

"I'm sorry," Brendon went on. "For making you worry."

She waited a moment, her eyes still holding his. She tightened the corners of her mouth and seemed about to speak. But she shrugged and turned away.

"I mean it," said Brendon. "I'm sorry."

She shrugged a second time, still not looking at him. Then she walked over to the Jeep.

"Thank you, Philip," she said.

"We're all very lucky," Philip said.

"I guess so," replied Anne, without enthusiasm. "I thought I could trust him to act responsibly."

Brendon shot Courtney a quick glance, and she caught it and gave him a nod. She seemed to be saying: Don't listen, don't worry, okay?

"Look," said Philip, "everybody's tired and the kids are still wet and cold. Why don't we wait till tomorrow to get to the bottom of this."

Anne said, "All right."

Philip asked, "Could you send Brendon over here?"

As his mother came for him, Brendon watched Philip Holmes open his door and step down.

"Philip wants to talk to you," Anne said.

"I heard," replied Brendon. He walked toward Philip, who wandered to the water's edge. When he stopped a good fifty feet from his Jeep, he turned around and waited for Brendon. The two of them were out of earshot.

Philip said, "Tell me, as rationally as you can, why you took Courtney along."

"She was *with* me," answered Brendon.

Philip Holmes stared off, pretended to scan the marina to his left.

"Talk to her about it," Brendon went on. "She'd like that."

"I plan to," said Philip, bringing his gaze back to Brendon.

"She saved my life."

"And nearly lost hers playing daredevil."

Brendon stood quietly.

"What do you expect me to say?" Philip pressed. "You want me to thank you for helping her so much?"

"She doesn't need my help," said Brendon.

Philip glared at Brendon, then cocked an eyebrow. "But she sure as hell could use mine. That the gist?"

Brendon shrugged.

"I'm trying hard to make sense of this," Philip said, gesturing toward the Jeep, the skiff. "And her. And you, for that matter."

Brendon averted his eyes.

"We'll talk tomorrow, maybe," said Philip.

Brendon nodded.

"Go home," said Philip.

Without further comment, Brendon turned and walked back toward his mother, passing her and going directly to the car. Once inside, he glanced at Anne. She looked at Philip, who gave her a curt nod before returning to his Jeep.

"What did he tell you?" asked Anne, closing her door. Ross slid quietly into the backseat, said nothing.

"Chewed me out."

Anne breathed deeply twice before saying, "The thought of losing another . . ." Her voice clogged and tears formed. She blinked them away, shaking her head.

"I know," said Brendon. "I thought it might get rough, but nothing like it was. We wanted to sail over and back."

Anne gazed at the steering wheel.

Ross asked, "When did it start raining? I mean, how far were you?"

Twisting around, Brendon said, "About halfway over. I'm not really sure."

"*Please!*" said Anne, grasping the wheel. "Don't start telling your war stories in front of me."

With that she fumbled her key into the ignition and started the car. The three of them rode away from the dock in grim silence.

• • •

Back at the cottage, Brendon showered and crawled into bed. He fell asleep as soon as he pulled the old afghan up to his shoulders.

19

When Brendon woke up, he had no idea what time it was. But he knew where he was and where he'd been.

He pushed away the covers and slid his legs off the bed. He wore only a T-shirt and running shorts. For a few moments he sat there in the darkness. He reached over and peeked behind the window shade. It was dark outside too.

But beneath the bedroom door, a thin bar of light shone. Brendon rose stiffly and shuffled toward it. He opened the door and found Ross reading on the couch in front of a small fire.

Craning his neck, Ross turned and said, "He is risen."

Glancing around, Brendon said, "Where's Mom?"

"She slept all afternoon too, but now she's at Beth Neal's."

"Why?"

"Why d'you suppose?!" said Ross. "You scared the heck out of her is why. She needs someone to talk to."

Brendon stared at his brother, who went right back to his magazine. Brendon walked over to the big leather chair and sat down.

"She about went nuts when they put it together," Ross continued, not looking at Brendon.

"Well, it's *still* together."

"That was really pretty *stupid*," Ross said in a tone so surly that Brendon flinched.

"Depends," he responded, trying for calm.

"Dad was enough, okay?" Ross turned his gaze on Brendon. "We don't need any more wildman crap. I can't take it."

Brendon looked closely at Ross. He was dead serious.

"Why'd you do that?" Ross asked, his eyes drilling into Brendon's now.

"You should know."

"Oh yeah? Well, I don't." Ross's hostility was growing.

"Because you had it easy," Brendon shot back.

"The hell does *that* mean? What're you talking about?"

"Dad. Your basketball."

Ross was silent. He looked more confused. Then he saw it. "You one-upped him," he said.

"I finished the job."

"That's why?!" he said loudly. "You nearly killed yourself just to cross the Door and beat him at something? I don't believe it!"

"Hey look, you *had* everything, okay?"

"And you didn't? You're *crazy*, Brendon!" Ross hollered. "You really don't know how he talked about you? What I had to hear?"

Brendon was taken aback. "Never talked to *me*," Brendon said finally.

"You don't always listen," Ross continued. "He said you were the best, a lot smarter than him even, smart enough to take care of yourself. With me, he thought I needed all the help I could get."

Brendon was shocked by Ross's words. He didn't know how to react, whether to laugh in his brother's face or cry into his own hands. Sure enough, Michael Turner had called it

true. The man knew his boys, and Brendon suddenly under-
stood that he'd just proved Michael was right about him. He
could take care of himself. He had gone to the edge, but he
was able to pull back just in time.

"You've got no chance alone," he said out loud.

"Thanks," said Ross, still upset.

"No," said Brendon. "I meant anybody, everybody. She
saved me out there."

Ross sat up, leaned toward Brendon, his brow lined with
furrows of amazement. "Courtney?"

"Yes."

"How?"

Brendon explained. And as he did he began to think about
her, their night in the shed, the closeness, the warmth.

Just then Ross touched Brendon's shoulder. Brendon
hadn't seen him rise, heard him cross the room.

"Don't ever do that again," Ross said, attempting to smile.
"Something crazy."

"I won't have to," said Brendon.

20

Courtney said, "We're going down to the dock, okay?"

Philip, seated on the couch, looked at her and smiled.

Brendon and Courtney walked out holding hands.

It was three days later and all of them—Anne, Ross, Philip, Courtney, and Brendon—had enjoyed a quiet dinner at Philip's cabin. The party was a Bon Voyage get-together for Courtney, who would be returning to Chicago in the morning.

Walking down the sloping yard, Brendon noticed the wind had picked up. It caught Courtney's white cotton sundress and molded it to her body.

She said, "The breeze will keep the bugs off."

They dropped hands when they reached the dock. They walked single file out to the end. There they were silent for a moment, hearing the waves, watching the stars. Brendon put his hand on her shoulder, and she reached up and touched his hand with her fingers. She said nothing, but continued to stare at the lake.

"I wish it was just starting," she said, squeezing his hand. "Knowing you."

"Isn't it?"

"Probably. Then it seems like it started a long time ago."

"There'll be other summers," said Brendon. "I bet my grandfather buys the Hawkins place."

"Maybe you'll come see me in Chicago this fall," she said quietly.

"Maybe."

"Maybe not?"

"I wonder if we'll be the same in Chicago. Maybe I won't be what you're used to."

"How could you know what I'm used to in Chicago? You been grilling Gambini again?" Courtney tilted her head so that she seemed to be looking down over her cheekbone at him.

"Unfortunately, his powers have limits. You're out of range down there."

"You sure he's not guilty of false advertising with that 'sees all, knows all'?"

"You're right, of course. Gambini's a fraud. I guess I knew it all along. But we still need him."

"Yeah?"

"The idea he *might have* such power keeps us on the straight and narrow."

"Gambini, Guru of Guilt."

"Something like that."

She was quiet a moment. Then, "What's the matter, Brendon?" she asked. "Don't you think visiting me would be fun?"

"What's 'fun'?"

"Doing what you like and not worrying about it," she answered quickly.

"Then visiting you would be fun."

"So you'll come down?"

". . . I don't know."

"You want me to say 'pretty please'?"

"You've never had to beg in your life."

"Please," she whispered, stepping even closer to him.

"You're kidding."

"No," she said. "I really have to see you again. I'm not going to be subtle or coy about it." She pressed against him, and he put his hands on either side of her face, thumbs near the corners of her eyes, fingers in her hair.

"I feel just like you. You know that," he said softly.

"So you'll come to Chicago?"

"I'll call you when I get home. We can maybe set a date."

"Brendon, I know we'll be okay together whenever we meet. We'll be able to talk even if we don't see each other for twenty years. We've been through something."

He nodded. "I get more scared remembering, thinking about what *could*'ve happened."

"Me too. But only sometimes."

"I'm just glad you're okay."

"C'mon," she said, pulling him by the wrist.

She led him to the shore, where she slipped off her sandals and let the cool waves slide around her ankles.

"You'll get your dress wet."

"I don't care," she said lightly. "Tonight I feel so good I think I'll *swim* to the mainland."

"Another time, okay?"

She laughed and came over to him, said, "I suppose we better go back inside."

"I suppose."

Instead of moving, though, she smiled warmly, then

reached around him and hugged him.

And he loved it.

• • •

The next morning Brendon woke up late to the gurgling of running water. Ross was in the bathroom. Courtney was on her way to Chicago.

Brendon rolled onto his back and stretched. Then he laced his hands together behind his head and thought about last night, and the last three weeks. *Running water,* he thought. He was through with running, he knew that now. But not with water . . . or islands. Far from it. For he felt a kinship to this island. It was his home now. He had earned a place here. He'd grown up here. That's what made it his home. And there was Courtney.

He let another few minutes pass before he climbed out of bed and wandered into the bathroom. There he found Ross, standing in his underwear in front of the small mirror.

"More growth?" said Brendon.

Ross gave him a sideways look. His face was covered with splotches of shaving cream, not a smooth coating.

"You doing blades yet?" Brendon asked.

"Absolutely."

"What's with the dab-dab approach?"

"It's Farber's idea."

"I thought so."

"He calls it 'spot work.' It's the last step before the total adult experience."

"Spot work."

"You get control of the obvious problem areas. Go after the tough ones first. Attack 'em. Break 'em down. Dominate 'em."

"That's an attitude," Brendon said thoughtfully.
"Huh?"
"That's a good attitude."
"For shaving."
"Lotta things."